JOURNEY INTO DANDELION WINE COUNTRY

JOURNEY INTO DANDELION WINE COUNTRY

And Other Different Stories

Alan Ira Gordon

ORD

To order additional copies of this book, contact:
Xlibris Corporation
1-888-7-XLIBRIS
www.Xlibris.com
Orders@Xlibris.com

CONTENTS

FOR RAY BRADBURY,
AND FOR SAM AND BEAU

There is a land of the living, and a land of the dead,
and the only bridge between them is love . . .
the ultimate survival.

-Thornton Wilder

Journey into
Dandelion Wine Country

1

When I was a little boy back in the late sixties, I loved a TV movie show that was broadcast on CBS every Friday evening. The show offered classic films to kids who were just reaching the age where they could appreciate such cinema. I cared not at all for the classic tales, of course. What I loved were the stories, which were good and interesting. In my favorite, which I watched three times from start to finish, Mel Ferrer is a self- pitying puppeteer with a French carnival. He takes in and cares for a poor orphan girl named Lili, played by Leslie Caron.

To me she represented everything that a coming-of-age French beauty should be. Tall and slender,with large brown eyes, short brunette hair, creamy white skin and a sweet, slender neck, she tempted me to lean into the screen and commence nibbling. With time, her reality has blurred in my memory into an ideal of perfect womanhood.

The picture itself was a musical. There was a song sung through-out about Lili, with a haunting refrain:

> A song of love is a song of hope/
> And that's the way that it goes/
> Hi Lili, Hi Lili, Hi Lo, Hi Lo/
> Hi Lili, Hi Lili, Hi Lo/
> Hi Lili, Hi Lili, Hi Lo Hi Lo/
> Hi Lili, Hi Lili (beat)/
> Hi Lo.

Back then my mother was young and beautiful. She had managed to keep most of her retired professional dancer's step about her.

As I sat alone in our theatre-darkened living room, watching the "Hi Lili" song, my mother would arrive from our kitchen. Damp dishtowel in hand, she would softly pirouette and jette across the theatre-dark living room, back and forth, over and over. The ghostly flickering blue glow of the old black-and-white screen lit her features from below, shedding the years and disappointments for albeit a brief, musical moment.

The scene would play itself out as my mother came to a graceful halt. She curtsied and silently glided back into the kitchen. We never spoke of her performance.

As the years grew, the memory stayed with us both. From time to time, my mother would softly sing the "Hi Lili" song as we went about the household; she would catch herself and halt as we both silently smiled in remembrance.

When I recall this childhood memory, I wish that I could also remember the title of that damn movie. I could go to the *Video King*, describe it to the girl behind the counter. But that would be the easy out, it wouldn't prove anything, it wouldn't be me. I have to somehow reach back into that childhood attic in the back of my head, somehow dust the title off and bring it down, all by itself, into the living room of my consciousness. My efforts of late at this mental exercise have proven frighteningly futile.

As have my efforts at convincing my mother that my own Lili ever lived.

2

I first met Lili Pepper in a dance class in the West End of London back in 1977, about a week after I left home. Living at home and going to college back in Massachusetts wasn't for me; like my mother before me, my feet lectured to me more impressively than any history professor ever could. I had four years of high school choreography under my belt, and had seen the Minelli-DeNiro screen version of *New York, New York* at least nine times. If I could make it there, I'd make it anywhere, right? Better yet, why not skip the there, and head directly to anywhere?

Young, cocky and sure to be a star of stage and screen, I cashed-in my savings bonds, thumbed my way eastward to Logan International Airport and bought a one-way British Airways ticket via Heathrow to the London Theatre District. It just seemed to have a more historical flavor to it than running off to Broadway.

From that first day in dance class, onward, Lili was my one and only sweetness. I couldn't stop watching her tall, slender frame assuredly move through her tight routines, straw blond hair wisping lightly astray, perspiration beading around and down her finely-chiseled back muscles. Musky perspiration drifted under my nostrils. All at once I tasted vanilla and honey, sex and love, caring and the sweet heartbursting ache of intense longing. Lili sensed me across the room as her number played out, demurely raised her azure-blue eyes to meet my hungered gaze. She smiled knowingly, nostrils steadily flaring as she toweled down, heading toward me.

She took me out that evening, obstensively to fill in a fellow American chorus hoofer on theatre life in the West End. She took me home with her later that night-to our home, a small, leaky flat off of Baker Street. It was unspoken, yet easily understood by both of us that Lili had claimed me for her own.

The next year was a pleasant, dream-like movie sequence, as Lili literally took me under her wing, for both professional and personal growth. I was mesmerized by her drive, her strong, out-going personality and desire to achieve. I suppose that she domi-nated and controlled me in most ways, but I was not very worldly, and at that stage in my young life I was very comfortable with the lopsided security of Lili leading the relationship.

She protectively dragged me around to a myriad of dance classes, acting and singing workshops. Casting calls would invari-ably find us together, as Lili nailed one or another supportive role that seemed cast just for her. I was very content to spend the time in Lili's professional shadow, easily ignoring the gossip and wimp jokes made by casting call rivals at my expense. Lili taught me more than any formal training program ever could about dance and show in general, but my own dancing ambition never fully jelled. I was only nineteen years old to Lili's show-toughened twenty-five, and for all intents and purposes sexually inexperienced. A high school relationship had included only one encumbering experience with lovemaking.

Lili went about that act of teaching me intimacy with her as fiercely and deeply as she taught me our profession. Before long, all that came to matter to me, all that I lived for, was making long, sweet love with Lili.

I was intensely overwhelmed that such a sexy, beautiful woman had chosen me to be so intimate with her, to enter her and share her body. Although everything about Lili was driven, she was so sweet and gentle in teaching me how to love her.

Having never considered myself handsome or even particu-larly good-looking, at first I felt very self-conscious about my body. Through touching and talking, and just being kind and giving, Lili and I together brought down that shield. She showed me so many sweet ways that I could touch, and taste, and hold to make her feel so good. The greatest please Lili ever gave me was in the joy she expressed in the taking of our intimacy.

The height of our love for each other peaked very early one morning, about a year after my arrival in London. It was around 4:00 in the morning and we had come home from a particularly raucus cast party full of lust and life for each other and were ardently coupling in our living room, lit only by a barely glowing fire.

I desperately loved and craved the texture of Lili's body, combined with the taste and natural scent of her as our lovemaking stretched out long, slow and sweetly. We reached this one, rare moment on that particular morning, our bodies covered with slick, musky sweat, wrapped so tightly around each other. As we both came together, everything about the moment seemed to compact naturally into one precious physical and emotional sensation, hurling itself directly to the center of my heart. Utterly overwhelmed, I buried my face in the sweet, cupped hollow between Lili's throat and shoulder, softly wept with love as I felt her dancer's thigh's still clasping tightly about my back, grasping desperately to hold the perfect moment.

It wasn't enough. I needed to give one more *something*, a touch or taste or word as a final expression of that once in a lifetime moment of mutually-reached bliss. It came out in old words. I softly kissed up to her sweet earlobe and whispered it:

"Hi Lili, Hi Lili . . . Hi Lo . . . "

Lili's sweet thighs relaxed as she gently reached over and took my face in her hands. She turned me to gaze at her eye-to-eye, slight inches apart, our faces and hair matted with the sweated aftermath of our love for each other. She kissed me softly and longer than she ever had before or ever would again. Then we gently dried each other off, and slept late into the English day.

3

There are notes between the keys that we don't hear.
                                        -Thelonius Monk

August, 1989

I walk the Tatnuck Village section of the city, the old neighborhood where I grew up, where my mother still lives. The
afternoon is cloudy and gray, yet sticky humid. I pass a seedy
bookstore, a bar named Chino's, a coffee house, scattered houses
in between.

I think of phone calls. Pictures. Letters.

Letters.

I turn around and go back a block, head northward up a
hilly sidestreet into a neighborhood of old Victorian houses.
The massive structures squat like tired burdens along the back-
side of the hill's twisting road. Thick lilac bushes grow upward
and out from each front yard. I bend forward to avoid the
overchoke of purple-coned lilacflowers and sweet scent hanging heavily above the sidewalk. Halfway up the hillside I turn
in, push my way along a narrow dirt path between protesting
bushes to reach the front porch.

The weathered Victorian is painted in various layers of somber
blue and gray, paint cracked and peeling through the overlaying
coats with the exception of the shiny blue porch. I walk up onto it,
ring the doorbell, place my left palm hesitantly against the outer
screen door. The heavy wood door scraps inward.

Colleen's face is surrounded by billowing cascades of soft, red hair, smiling green eyes awash in a sea of light freckles. She wears light blue shorts and a faded yellow U Mass t-shirt.

Through the screen, the years melt away.

Colleen and I face each other on her screened-in back porch. We are seated on a pair of heavy, wooden wicker porch lounges spray-painted white, the original undercoating peeking through the arm-rests in streaks of dried blood red. Atop a small card table, boxes overflow with stacks of soft-cover books. I recognize nothing, but from high school I am sure that most are science fiction or fantasy.

We sip a cool mix of lemonade and bourbon from thick paper cups, glance often out at the small backyard abuzz with the midafternoon drone of fat yellow and black bumblebees drifting amongst purple cones. A carrot-topped toddler contentedly coos wrapped around Colleen's bare feet, asprawl amongst and assort-ment of Transformers and Lego pieces.

She apprises me from above the rim of her cup, Irish eyes asmile.

"I knew you'd eventually drop by, Guy." She laughs good-naturedly. "What took so long? Afraid of meeting Roy?"

I laugh back. She knows I only fear myself.

"I've been preoccupied, lately."

"So I've heard. Mothers talk."

Colleen's soft, rust lashes cast downward as she bends over toward the toddler and replaces a sharp-edged Transformer with a soft gray teddybear. The replacement seems to meet his satisfaction.

"Tell me what's going on, Guy."

I tell her everything.

I am succinct and to the point, eleven minutes flat. I summa-rize my twelve good months with Lili, 1977. I skate across the thin emotional ice of the following months in 1978, the bad ones. I try but can't keep my lower lip from trembling when I talk of the decline, the final, emotionally drowning ache. But I do hold up better than expected. I manage to say "leukemia" the three times when required without stammering.

Four minutes flat. Good job.

I continue with the Tampa supper club gig six months after the funeral, outline my moves over the ensuing years. Houston to L.A. To off-Broadway to New Haven, to etcetera and back. Always alone, always the journeyman dancer/actor/singer/whatever. Until two weeks ago. When I finally came home to Massachusetts, to take some stock of it all.

The overdue reunion with my mother is emotional, but do-able for both of us. There was only one problem.

She didn't remember Lili.

I ended up calling Doctor Howard, my New York therapist. She was on vacation.

I summarize for Colleen on schedule. Time to move on to the topic of logic.

"I don't know, maybe it's a brain thing, but I don't think so-my mother seems physically o.k. But she swears to the bottom of her soul that I never lived with Lili in London!"

Colleen listens with a look of calm concentration.

"Look, I know I've been away too long. I had to. A big chunk of me died with Lili, and the rest of me just wasn't ready to crawl back here. She's my only relative, my mom, and we're alike, so she understood. If I came back here to lick my wounds, I'd have to totally face what happened to Lili. I couldn't do that, so I fled from show to show."

I tense more, begin to slowly rub my hands over and around each other.

"I . . . I wrote a lot. We sent each other stuff, we talked on the phone from time to time."

"About what?" As if the question needs to be asked.

"About anything *but* Lili, for Christ's sake!"

I struggle not to shout. "I spent eleven years avoiding my mother on the phone about my Lili!"

Colleen waits. I breath deep and continue.

"My therapist, Doctor Howard. Lots of conversations there about the hurt being all I had left of Lili. She said I was fearful of letting my pain go by talking about it with my mother and anyone else back here."

"Like me."

I breathe deep. "Like you. We . . . finally got to the point where I could come back here and face how you guys might bring up Lili."

I feel drained, and stop. I wait.

"And?" Colleen prompts.

"And no one remembers Lili! Christ, my mom was proud of my London days, she told the neighbors, even the goddamn milkman about the two of us over there! So I finally come back and I'm ready to face-up to talking about Lili and she looks at me like I'm from Mars! We fight, I start calling people that she's told me over the years expressed sympathy, and none of them know about Lili and me-they think I'm over the edge!"

Colleen silently refills my bourbon and lemonade as the late afternoon light begins its slow dim. The toddler has unwrapped himself from around her legs and is curled up asleep by himself on the floor.

I drain the drink in a few quick gulps.

"Do you think I'm crazy?"

Colleen's features soften. "You're no more crazy now than we both were in high school." She shakes her head again. "Maybe something is wrong with your mother's memory. I just don't know how to explain away the other people not remembering your Lili."

She picks up the toddler, who continues gently snoring on her shoulder. "Ray and I only moved back here last year. I haven't seen your mother or her circle of friends since we dated in high school, until I heard a bit about you last week."

Now is the time to ask it. I press my empty cup flat between both palms."What about you?"

Freckles furrow in puzzlement. "Me?"

"Yeah, you. I sent you a letter about Lili."

Colleen pauses in rocking the toddler. "When?"

"About a month after she died. I didn't know your address up at U Mass so I mailed it to your mother with a note asking her to forward it."

We sit in silence. The backyard is quiet; the bees are tired, now.

"You've forgotten about Lili. And the letter's gone."

Colleen leans forward, long wisps of red hair lightly brush my hand. "That's not true, Guy. I never got the letter. Either it got lost in the mail or my mother threw it out."

"Ask her."

"She's old now, Guy, she'd never remember. It's been a long time."

I stand. "Look for the letter. It's somewhere here. Check the attic."

"Even if I had received the letter, what makes you think I'd still have it?"

"I know you. You would have kept it. Always."

Colleen looks up and our eyes lock for long seconds.

I turn to go. Colleen rises with her tiny slumberer on her shoulder, follows me through the house out onto the front porch. As I turn to say goodbye she moves forward and quickly kisses me softly on the lips.

I look down at the baby. "Colleen."

"Yes, Guy?"

"Did you ever tell Ray about . . . us in high school?"

"That night?"

I nod.

She softly touches my cheek. "Yes, I did."

I look back up, my lower lip beginning to betray me yet again. Her loving look calms me.

"Guy, sometimes it's okay to dig up the past and share it with someone else."

I smile tentatively. "It helps one face the future, right?"

"No," she says softly. "It helps one to live in the present."

I walk down the steps and head toward the street. Halfway down the path Colleen calls to me. "Guy?"

I turn.

"Come back some evening. I'd really like you to meet Ray.

"I will."

"Oh, and Guy?"

I wait.

"Keep trying to get through to Doctor Howard, okay? And let me know." With a reassuring smile, she turns and heads back into the house as the toddler awakens and begins to cry.

4

I squint through the morning sun's glare into the coffee shop window, searching for Colleen. Giving up, I fumble semi-blind through the doorway and pause inside.

She is waiting for me at a corner table off to the back. The toddler in her lap recognizes me. "Hi ninny, hi no-o-o . . . " he burbles in greeting around a well-sucked thumb. I sit before a cup of tea that Colleen has ordered for me.

Her long hair is gathered up in a working knot, loose strands randomly haloing about. She looks haggard, with her eyes puffy, cheeks mottled red. And something else.

She looks scared.

She reads the thought in my eyes, rapidly shakes her head no.

"I've stayed away from the bourbon and lemonade since your visit."

"Then what is it?"

She looks down, plays nervously with the string from a discarded tea bag crumpled on a side saucer. "I believe you."

"That's nice."

"I also think I know why no one remembers Lili."

"Enlighten me."

Colleen looks up sharply, holds her breath lightly, then makes a decision.

"It's you, Guy."

"Me."

She shifts the baby in her lap, continues while eyeing me carefully. "Maybe I read too much, but I think that you've made everyone forget."

She waits for me to protest.

I say nothing.

Colleen leans forward, her tone urgent. "Don't you see, somehow your subconscious fear of people confronting you with Lili's death made them forget her, made the pictures and letters go away! Deep down inside you're relieved that you don't have to complete your walk through the valley of Lili's death."

She gives me a very hard stare. "A walk that began eleven years ago. A walk that should end, now."

As Colleen speaks I have been balling up tiny pieces of torn paper napkin. I now brush them aside. "It's a neat fantasy, Colleen. It really is. Whether it's true or not won't matter much longer." I am out of tea and my mouth is very dry.

"Guy, I-"

"I called Doctor Howard, just before you phoned me."

"And?"

I swallow with some difficulty. "And she doesn't remember Lili." This time it looks as if even Colleen's baby eyes me with fear. "She says that we've never talked about a Lili Pepper, and that all of our sessions dealt with my being lonely. She suggests that we get together about this as soon as I get back to New York."

"It's getting worse."

I stare numbly.

"Don't you see," Colleen hisses. "You're spreading it! First your mother, then her friends and me, now Doctor Howard; you've got to make a conscious effort to move on!"

A sudden thought occurs. "If I made you forget about Lili, why do you believe me now?"

Colleen's weary eyes take on a glitter of anticipation. "I haven't been able to sleep since you left the other day. I keep thinking about it, everything you said." She reaches down to the toddler, gently raises up his arms from beneath the tabletop. Clutched in one tiny fist is a crumpled envelope. She plucks it from his hand, waves it triumphantly. "Don't you see, you wanted me to find it-you told me to look in the attic! Part of you is fighting to get through this; it kept this letter alive! Even though my memory of it was erased, you wanted me to get it!"

She holds the envelope out in offering and sighs. "That's an off-beat mental power you got there, buck-o."

The envelope is creased and yellowed with the passage of aching years; I recognize my jagged, tense handwriting from those painful days. A purple Queen's visage British stamp embosses the upper right-hand corner. God Save The Queen, echoes as a dull thought in my head.

I lightly cup the envelope in the palms of both hands, as if it were a dying baby bird. Lili's heartbeat weakly pulses outward from the words through the battered envelope, tickling my skin. My eyes blur.

"Did you read it again?" The sobbing starts.

"Yes." A blurred hand moves to her mouth. "Oh, Guy . . . "

"I miss her so much." I can't stop crying, heavy tears pattering down on the envelope. The coffee shop becomes very quiet. I am only afraid of scaring Colleen's toddler.

I hear approaching footsteps. A man clears his throat, asks Colleen if I am okay. She provides reassurances, as if she is talking about a child.

I still can't stop crying, must fight to catch breath. Her chair softly scrapes back. Clothing rustles about; a moment, and Colleen eases the envelope from my cradled hands and places her toddler in my lap. Through a rainbowed blur I see his little round face staring up in wide-eyed, purely innocent wonderment. Chubby fingers reach up, softly rub the wetness on my cheeks. "Hi No-o-o . . . Hi No-o-o . . . " he whispers, mesmerized.

It works. After a few moments, I am breathing steadily and seeing clearly. The baby loses interest. With thumb in mouth, he leans his head against my chest and closes his eyes.

I look up at Colleen, again seated across from me. She is placing the letter in her purse, removing in kind a wad of tissue. She holds it out, her face awash with a mixture of pride and caring. "Feel better?"

I nod, take the tissue and use it.

"That's good," Colleen murmers. "A good first step."

"I don't know what to do next. I can't face letting her go."

"Guy MacKenzie, you listen to me good. If you don't somehow stop doing whatever it is you're doing, it's only gonna get worse."

"How could things get any worse than they are, now?"

"Guy, I . . . I just think that erasing Lili from everyone around here was just a first misstep. The more you stay emotionally frozen over time, the worse it's gonna get. Today you reached out and erased Lili from Doctor Howard." She pauses, her emerald eyes widening. "What if tomorrow you called Indianapolis and no one out there remembered Lili? How could you do that to her? They're her family, the people who knew and raised her and loved her as a child. Lili has to be remembered by them, whoever they are. And by you."

"Me." I whisper.

"Yes, you." She reaches out, grasps my hand. "If you don't stop it, you could wake up some morning soon and not remember her, yourself."

I feel dizzy for a moment. Colleen's hand squeezes mine, steadying. The feeling passes.

"I know that you're afraid of abandoning the past because of your love for Lili. But think about this, Guy. You need the good memories of Lili to be with you in the years ahead. And Lili needs to be remembered by you. In a strange way, you've got to let her go, to genuinely keep her."

I look at her pleadingly.

Colleen gathers up her stuff. We both stand as she reaches over for the baby. "You'll find a way. It's just another form of love, that's all." She smiles broadly. "You can work real hard to find love and nothing happens. Then when you least expect it, you just turn around and it's standing right there, just waiting for you."

She puts her arm through mine. "C'mon, it's close enough to noon. I'll buy you a bourbon and lemonade in Chino's."

I sit on a barstool facing a mahogany bar in Chino's. Colleen has had a quick ginger ale to my bourbon and lemonade. After mutual assurances, she gathers up baby to leave. "Hi ninny, hi no-o-o," he coos in farewell.

She suddenly pauses. "Lili."

"Huh?"

She laughs. "What he just said. Hi Lili, Hi Lo. It's from that movie called Lili."

"Lili." I turn the name over on my tongue very slowly, staring at myself in the mirror across the bar. "It's so simple. Why couldn't I ever remember the name?"

"Sometimes something you're looking for just pops up, when you least expect it."

I turn to Colleen and the baby. They are both smiling at me. Deep in my gut I know that a step has just been taken. I know for certain that whenever I finally get around to walking back into my mother's parlor, there will be a small, gilt-framed picture standing on the table near the window.

A picture of Lili and me. In it we are both laughing.

And dancing.

5

Why and how? Because I say it is so.

-Ray Bradbury, Dandelion Wine

June, 1991

I have not been on an airplane for over two years, and have quickly come to regret breaking my aeronautic boycott. US Air Flight 346 is crowded, stuffy and bumpy. Flight 101 out of Boston was tolerable. Flight 346 out of Des Moines is beginning to chafe.

The rotund businessman with whom I share an armrest in Economy Class decides to make polite conversation.

"You out here for business, pleasure or family, son?"

I hesitate a moment. "Family-sort of." Another hesitation. "Girlfriend's family."

The businessman chuckles, his Midwestern features spreading into a Babbit-wide smile.

"Ah, yes . . . meeting the girlfriend's family. Can be either a sweet dream or a sour nightmare."

The pilot's intercom voice interrupts my seatmate's musing.

"Ladies and gentlemen, we'll be ascending another 3000 feet to get out of this turbulence, things should smooth-out in about five minutes. If you look out the left side of the plane, you'll see that we're passing just about south of Green Town, Illinois. We'll be flying over Gary, Indiana in about twenty minutes, after which we'll be cleared to head southeasterly into Indianapolis. We should touchdown in about an hour."

Several rows forward a young, red-haired boy, no more than seven years old, stands up and steps into the aisle. He turns to face the tail end of the plane, arms spread-out wide in command. In a strong voice seemingly beyond his few years, he launches into song:

"Gary, Indiana! Gary, Gary Indiana! Gary, Indiana . . . "

My thoughts turn to Robert Preston, the Midwestern Music Man himself, and the good people of River City. My faithful businessman companion loudly chuckles and nods in tune, clearly enjoying himself and the boy.

"He looks just like the tyke in the movie! What was his name, now?" He snaps his fingers loudly in remembrance. "Opie Cunningham! That's it, yeah!"

"You're wrong."

His head stops nodding, brow clouding with confusion. "Say again, son?"

"I'm afraid you're thinking of little Ronny Howard. After 'The Music Man,' he went on to play Opie Taylor on *The Andy Griffith Show*, and then Ritchie Cunningham on *Happy Days*." I smile real friendly. "You just mixed your metaphors a bit, is all."

The clouds across my neighbor's brow begin to break. "Darned if you aren't right, son, now that I remember it! Funny how easy it is to forget something so simple!" He shakes his head and laughs pleasantly. "I'd lose my own head if it wasn't screwed onto my neck!"

"Gary, Indiana! Gary, Gary Indiana!" The boy pirouettes and jettes about the aisle, awhirl with preadolescent ease. "Gary, Indiana! Gary, Gary Indiana!"

The plane suddenly hits a small air pocket, not enough to even affect the boy's presence of command, but enough to splash that sinking, elevator-drop feeling down into the pit of my stomach.

I think about the dream, and this trip . . . the helpless anxiety of it all rises like a new bile in my throat. I turn wide-eyed to my faithful companion.

"There's trouble," I blurt out. "Here in River City . . . with a capital 'E' and that rhymes with 'P' and that spells Eleanor Pepper."

The businessman from Indianapolis has absolutely no idea what I'm babbling about. He stares at me for a moment, then brightens as he misapplies my thought to his earlier comment.

"There, there now, son!" He pats my shoulder reassuredly with a beefy hand. "It's no trouble at all, forgetting an occasional actor's name." He winks and laughs. "Im just getting a little more middle-aged than I was! A little forgetfulness could never kill no one. It ain't like a death, or nothin'."

The young boy's commanding arms seem to be reaching out toward me, as his voice takes on a huskier, more earnest tone.

"Gary, Indiana! Gary, Gary, Indiana!"

Lili was the real leading actor. I was just a boy in the chorus. I give up the diversion as the boy completes his performance and bows to scattered applause.

In the dream, I am lying on my back in bed, naked, arms stiffly by my sides. Soft moonlight filters through the window, gently illuminating my bedroom.

I am swathed in sweat and terror.

A soft clicking noise and the bedroom door breezes open. I open my eyes.

Eleanor Pepper stands naked in the doorway. A younger face than her sister Lili, but the same straw-blond hair and bright blue eyes, strong Pepper cheekbones and slender, sensuous body. The soft moonlight bathes her pert breasts, illuminating large nipples, turning soft blond pubic hair aglow with reflected dreamlight.

She saunters toward the bed, chest thrust out with arrogant confidence. I struggle but cannot move. I lie helpless and embarrassed, staring at Eleanor as I sport a large erection. She halts standing over me, a leer painting her face, holding my bedtime gym shorts wadded-up in her right hand. "I think I'll hang onto these as a little nighttime souvenir." Eleanor's eyes travel from my expression down my body, finally resting on my crotch.

She bends over me and grasps my erection with her free hand. She laughs as I gasp-that deeply seductive, husky Pepper-woman's laugh.

"Hey, Guy."

My eyes lock on her face. I gasp deeper, breathe more raggedly. Our eyes stay locked as Eleanor's hand moves about, a blur in the corner of my vision.

Eleanor works faster. I arch my back and peak, crying out in orgasm as Eleanor tosses her head back and roars with husky laughter. She leans in, her face a mere inch from mine.

She speaks, her voice a deeply menacing instrument.

"Come on out here and listen to the heartbeat of Middle America, *Boogie Boy* . . . and I'll let Cecil and Barbara Anne remember you. And if you're a good Boogie Boy, I'll let *all* of you remember big sister Lili. Ashes to ashes, fun to funky . . . "

Eleanor grins and licks the tip of my nose as I wake up.

Trouble in River City.

I awake naked, dried semen on my thigh. After doning underwear, I spend the next half-hour searching my apartment for the gym shorts I had worn to bed the night before. I never find them.

With trembling fingers, I dial-up my good friend Colleen, who quickly comes over and can't find them, either. We spend the morning drinking half a fifth of bourbon with a quart of lemonade. Then I call Cecil and Barbara Anne.

Sweet dreams and sour nightmares.

6

US Air Flight 346 actually touches down at the Indianapolis International Airport five minutes ahead of schedule. I bid my traveling companion goodbye, smile at the young pseudo-Ronny Howard as he waits with his folks at the baggage carousel. At the National Car Rental counter I pick-up the keys for a blood-red Geo Prizm.

The rental clerk asks me my destination, attempts to give friendly directions upon my answer.

"No need, thanks," I reply. "I've been here before."

Compared to driving in New England, the Indianapolis metropolitan area road network and traffic signage is a dream. In less than an hour, I have worked my way westward out of the city, easing the Geo Prizm past the Indianapolis Motor Speedway onto Route 36 west, then heading south on 231, winding my way south of Mansfield Lake.

I am heading for the rural countryside outside the town of Greencastle.

I am heading into the heart of dandelion wine country.

It is late afternoon when I reach my destination. I direct the rented car through swarming seas of elm and oak and maple, onto a red-bricked driveway growing off of a cracked country road. I park at the end of the driveway before a large, gray-and-white Victorian home in the midst of an emerald lawnscape. A matching gray-and-white barn sits nearby. Blond wheat fields and scattered orchards fade into the distance. I smell ten thousand chickens, and apples, peaches and midnight plums.

As I kill the engine and get out of the car, heavy footsteps pound down stairs from within the house. A pause, and the front screen door flings open, slamming hard against the house front. Though the door is quick on the rebound, Cecil Pepper clears the screen door's recoil and bounds down the front steps two-at-a-time.

Cecil is a large, beefy Midwestern man, a City Of Big Shoulders unto himself, with short blond hair, a twinkle in his pale blue eyes and a rosiness to his round cheeks.Lili used to say that her father Cecil was the long-lost twin brother of Alan Hale, who played the skipper on *Gilligan's Island*. Cecil is wearing his ever-present navy ensign's cap, a tradition brought back from a younger Cecil's hitch in the U.S. Navy.

He halts just short of the car, affixes me with excited eyes and childlike grin, then quickly takes a deep breath; holding his right hand palm-open with his left fist conducting a beat, Cecil sings in a rich, basso profundo voice:

> "My father was the keeper of the Eddystone Light,
> He slept with a mermaid one fine night,
> And from that union there came three,
> A porpoise, a piglet and the other was *me*!
> Ah-ha-ha, the wind blows free!
> My father was the Keeper of the Eddystone Light!"

Cecil springs forward, engulfing me in a deep bear hug, then releases me with a hearty laugh. "An old New England sea chanty for our young New England visitor! Welcome to our home, Guy!"

"You're looking good, Cecil."

He slaps his girth with both hands. "*Fit* as a fiddle, my boy, *fat* as a bass fiddle!"

The screen door beckons my attention anew with a steady, demure creak. I turn, and Barbara Anne frames the doorway in plain print dress and apron, a pair of low shoes in one hand and a dish towel in the other.

Barbara Anne needs little physical description. Suffice to say, she is Lili in late-middle age . . . a tall, blondish-graying Midwestern girl, aging as sweetly and strongly as a high, good bottle of dandelion wine. From shoes in hand, I gaze down to Barbara Anne's bare feet; they are good, rural Indiana feet, corn-nurtured and field-toughened, sculpted by the stuff upon which Hamlin Garland and Booth Tarkington based entire volumes of short stories.

They are Lili's feet.

I reluctantly break my footward gaze to greet Barbara Anne. She smiles a crinkly-eyed, warm caring smile in return; not for the first time, I feel as if Barbara Anne can read my thoughts.

"It's good to see you again, Guy." That husky, Pepper-woman voice.

"You too, Barbara Anne."

She nods knowingly toward the waiting porch swing, beckons me forward with a slight wave of fingers. Long, tapering Midwestern fingers. Lili's fingers.

"Sit with me a moment, while I catch my breath." She looks beyond me. "Cecil Pepper, take Guy's suitcase upstairs while we chat."

"Aye-aye, Skipper!"

Cecil gives me his own knowing nod as he easily hefts my suitcase across the porch. "After dinner, Guy, I expect you to give me a full debriefing of your New England seaside visits, of late!"

"Aye-aye, Skipper!"

A delighted wink and Cecil is gone.

I turn and watch as Barbara Anne gently slips on her shoes. She stretches her legs out before her, feet just above the porch floor, wiggling her toes through the open-toe flats.

We turn toward each other. I am a hell of a lot more comfortable at this moment than I thought I'd be.

It really is good to see the both of you again, Barbara Anne."

She smiles anew. "The feeling's mutual, Guy-from both Cecil and me." Barbara Anne takes on a wistful look, gazing off toward the distancing fields. "It's been so many years since you were last here."

"About thirteen."

"Thirteen years . . . " Barbara Anne almost whispers, incredulous. "It seems like almost yesterday." She turns toward me and places a strong hand over mine. Her eyes mist over, lost in time. "Like a very bad almost yesterday."

My own eyes fill as I bite my lower lip, work to breathe down steady. "I . . . I had to leave early. I couldn't help it."

The mist quickly clears from Barbara Anne's eyes as she watches me; a silent call has sounded between us, summoning forth Barbara Anne's home-grown nurturing instincts-through my memories, one of her own is in pain and sorrow. She pats my hand reassuredly.

"It was all right. The funeral was hard on all of us." She stands and folds her arms, gazing down at me proudly.

"For so long we heard nothing from you. Then two years ago you called . . . and we called back, once a month, back and forth."

She smiles wider. "And here you are! I'm so glad you're able to stay with us while you audition-which club in the city is the show at?"

I stand to face Barbara Anne. "When I called yesterday, I guess I told a bit of a white lie. There really isn't any show in Indy for me to audition for."

When we had settled into being a couple, there was a sixth sense between Lili and me-I'm sure it's common in a lot of folks who've been together awhile. Lili instinctively knew the moment before, when I was just about to bring-up a touchy subject.

The apple didn't fall far from the tree.

Barbara Anne doesn't even utter an "oh?" or a "then why are you here?"My answer is sitting there in her eyes, waiting on me . But I say it anyway.

"I'm really just here to see Eleanor."

Seven words that have the effect of ice water thrown on a warm, friendly fire. The twinkle dissolves into acrid smoke in Barbara Anne's eyes as her jaw hardens-not in anger, or defiance, but rather into a hurtful, protective stance. There is, after all, only one daughter left to her.

"Well, now," she says softly, distantly. "I think you were right the first time, Guy. You *are* here for an audition-of an entirely different kind from what you're used to, I'm afraid."

Barbara Anne's words and pained look chill me to the core, dripping as they are with a feeling of bleak inevitability. Cecil's voice beckons from above. "All's shipshape in the First Mate's cabin, Skipper!"

The moment breaks, and the old Barbara Anne returns. She happily turns and heads for the front door. "Well, I've got a fine welcome dinner planned for you, Guy! And I'd best get to it, less we're plannin' to eat at midnight!"

I blankly watch Barbara Anne's heels follow her feet into the house; the screen door slams hard, snapping me back into my pre-flight anxiety.

7

Barbara Anne has prepared a splendid Middle American farm dinner in honor of my arrival-roast chicken, potatoes, an array of steaming vegetables, the works. The three of us are seated in the airy dining room; a soft evening breeze rustles through the window screen, ruffling the fur on two farm cats patiently pacing about the room in wait for dinner scraps.

Cecil is delighted for the pleasure of my company, in his own inimitable way."More brussels sprouts, First Mate?" He holds forth for my reconsideration a steaming tray of the remaining vegetables.

"Thanks, Cecil, but I'm about ready to burst-everything was so good!"

Barbara Anne smiles appreciatively.

"Well now, son, there's always room for more brussels sprouts-they're so light and airy! You know what they say on that old t.v. commercial!"

Cecil daintily picks-up a round brussels sprout from his plate, rolls it in his palm and pops it into his mouth. He holds his palm outward for my inspection. "Melts in your mouth! Not in your hand!" He roars with delighted laughter; Barbara Anne and I cannot help but join in.

Barbara Anne waves a finger at Cecil in mock exasperation. "Now, Cecil Pepper, how many times have I told you not to play with your food!"

Cecil impishly covers his mouth. "Oops! Looks like I'm on K.P. Duty tonight, for sure!"

Barbara Anne stands and begins to stack dishes. "Some other night-tonight I need to feel busy. You boys just sit and have coffee."

Cecil and I are chatting about New England beaches when Barbara Anne calls out from the kitchen. "You gonna ride down to the State Fair with us tomorrow, Guy?"

"State Fair? I didn't know it was this week."

"You know what they say about the Indiana State Fair, don't you?" Before I can reply, Cecil is on his feet, *basso profundo* voice and metronome left hand at the ready:

> "Our State Fair is a *great* State Fair!
> Don't miss it! Don't even be late!
> It's dollars-to-donuts that our State Fair,
> Is the *best* State Fair in our state!"

I applaud appreciatively. "Very good, Cecil! The original cast of 'State Fair' couldn't have sung it better!"

Cecil beams with pride. "Thank you, my boy, thank you! It's always been my favorite musical! Let's do another one!" He pauses, looks at me quizzically. "You must have a favorite musical that we can sing to! What might that be, son?"

From the kitchen, all sounds of washing and rinsing cease. Both Barbara Anne and I collectively hold our breathes for a moment. Then I slowly let go. I cannot lie to avoid it. Not here. I speak quietly.

"My favorite musical is Lili, Cecil. I'm sure you remember it . . . with Leslie Caron and Mel Ferrer."

The smile runs away from Cecil's face. He sits heavily back down at the table, shoulders slumped. I guiltily wait as he removes his ensign's cap and runs his fingers through thinning hair.

"Yeah sure, Guy," Cecil mumbles. He stares past me, eyes lost in remembrance. "Lili . . . you don't think I'd really forget now, would you?" His face suddenly looks lined and tired. Momentarily stripped of the energetic merriment and mirth, I see what lies deep and still within-a worn Indianapolis insurance salesman retired in late-middle age to a small exurban farm, bearing the twin burdens of a long-dead daughter and another daughter in some kind of internal trouble. I sit before him swathed in my silent guilt, the phantom image of a probable son-in-law, had a kinder fate chosen to be less particular in its misfortunes.

The moment folds into itself as Barbara Anne presses through the swinging kitchen door, preceded by her special warmth.

"Well now, boys, seems like I could use some assistance, after all! Guy, why don't you help me dry?" She picks up Cecil's ensign's cap and afixes it firmly atop his head, tapping the brim straight. "And *you*, Cecil Pepper! I'm sure you've got some work to get to in your den!"

The light floods back into Cecil's frame. "That I do, Skipper, *that I do*!" We both follow Barbara Anne back into the kitchen. "There are VCR tapes to watch-episodes of Nightline and 60 Minutes to catalogue! My collection must stay up-to-date and organized!" With a wink and a nod, Cecil disappears into his den. I begin to dry and stack damp dishes aside Barbara Anne as she continues washing. From the direction of the den, television news show sounds float into the kitchen.

"I'm . . . I'm sorry, Barbara Anne. I didn't mean to upset him."

"Nothing to be sorry about, Guy. I tolerate Cecil's eccentricities-at times, I guess I even encourage'em . . . " We have fallen into a steady rhythm: Barbara Anne washes, rinses, then hands off to me for drying. "Sometimes, a person just has to be . . . forced to look into their own heart, look at their own pain and grief in order to get beyond it and continue livin' . . . and some people . . . well, they just sometimes put it off too long. You know what I mean, don't you?"

Barbara Anne's hands pause in the suds, waiting.

I am a show person, albeit an obscure one. I need no further lead-in. My cue has been spoken: enter, stage left.

"Where is Eleanor, Barbara Anne?"

Her hands hide very still in the diminishing soap suds.

"Cecil and I will be leaving very early in the morning for the State Fair. I'll leave you written directions on the kitchen table to reach Ellie, for when you wake up."

We recommence our washing rhythm and finish the remaining dishes in silence.

Tired from the journey, I ask Barbara Anne to say goodnight to Cecil for me. Padding quietly past the den, I spy Cecil within. He sits comfortably back in a worn lounger, remote control in one hand, pen in the other; Ted Koppel whirs about the TV screen in fast forward, as Cecil hastily scribbles labeling notes.

As I head up, Barbara Anne suddenly calls after me from the foot of the stairs.

"Guy?"

I pause and turn, then wait.

She hesitates a moment. "You never called Eleanor to tell us you were coming, did you?"

"No . . . I didn't."

We stare at each other a moment, no need for further words, now. I feel a slight stirring of relief; there is a tentative, yet hopeful support, here.

"Guy?"

"Yes?"

She speaks softly. "Thank you for coming. I hope you have a good sleep, to rest you for tomorrow."

Barbara Anne turns and disappears from my view. I continue upward, to the third-story cupola bedroom where my suitcase is set at the foot of a bed. There is a skeleton key in the door, which I turn to securely lock before retiring for sleep.

8

In the morning I awaken to find Cecil and Barbara Anne long
gone to the State Fair. After bidding good morning to a farm hand,
I fire-up the Geo Prizm and begin to follow Barbara Anne's written directions toward Eleanor.

The directions are very precise, listed in measured miles and
left-right turns, highway exits and occasional intersections. The
trip itself is not that far, really-back north on 231, then eastward
on Route 36, until I exit onto a sidestreet in a rural-suburban area
just outside the fringes of Indianapolis proper.

I spend a good fifteen minutes guiding the Geo Prizm up-
and-down St. James Street. None of the scattered house numbers
match the number where Eleanor is living. Turning onto West Ra-
vine, I seek direction at a Seven-Eleven convenience store. The Pakistani store clerk looks-up from Barbara Anne's directions with large,
sad eyes; he explains to me what Eleanor's parents could not face.

Back onto St. James Street, about two blocks down, take a left
at the grey-and-white sign. Follow the tree-lined driveway up the
rolling hillside, park anywhere on the right.

I find it in a minute-and-a-half, but idle the car at the driveway entrance for a good five minutes, staring at the grey-and-white
sign. Its Midwestern honesty has momentarily taken me aback.

Back in New England, it would have proclaimed a more so-
cially correct name, such as Byzantium-On-The-Hill, or Byzantium
Greencastle. Here in Indiana the name is disarmingly straightfor-
ward: "Byzantium Sanatorium."

Doctor Andreus Porcus sits opposite me behind his office desk, 230 pounds of sweating, disheveled flab packed into a too-tight white physician's jacket. Doctor Andy has cracked open a fresh bottle of Stolichnaya vodka and is steadily emptying its contents into a shot glass labeled "Best In The Midwest."

Doctor Andy breathes in short, shallow breaths from a small, pursed mouth set in a flush face, all topped by an unruly expanse of brown curls. His hand shakes as he pours himself the latest refill.

"I appreciate the time taken from your busy schedule to see me."

Doctor Andy presses the emptied shot glass against his flushed brow in a feeble attempt to cool down his heated anxiety. "Oh, no bother . . . no bother. Byzantium is fairly empty, right now . . . little for me to see to on a moment-by-moment basis. We're shutting down, actually. Consolidating with a larger, for-profit sana- . . . institute east of the city."

He release a goodly portion of his fear with a high-pitched, nervous laugh. "Actually, given the . . . personal nature of the situation, I was glad to oblige."

"Personal?"

He clumsily screws the metal cap back onto the vodka bottle. "I was a high school friend of . . . Eleanor's deceased sister."

"Lili."

Doctor Andy nods nervously, folds pudgy fingers before him on the desk. His features further soften into remembrance. "Best friend a fat boy ever had. When we were freshmen, tomboy Lili actually beat-up a junior boy who kept calling me 'Andy Porky.' "

I fondly laugh. "Yeah, I can remember that side of her."

Doctor Andy focuses on me from deep within his remembrance, eyes questioning.

"I was-"

"I know who you are!" His abruptness startles both of us. Face flushing anew, Doctor Andy reaches for the vodka bottle.

I place my hand over the empty shot glass. "Enough, Andrew." He pauses, staring longingly at the glass. "I need answers. First of all, why is Eleanor here?"

He looks at me with genuine surprise. "Why, because she wants to be here."

"Bullshit. Do you allow anyone who wants to run away from their problems to hide in Byzantium?"

Doctor Andy slowly affixes his gaze on me, face no longer flushed, his voice an icy clinical calm. "Do you dream much, Guy? Do you ever have uncommonly realistic sweet dreams? Or maybe sour nightmares?"

He correctly reads my reaction, takes strength from its obvious answer. Doctor Andy stands and turns, gazes through the blinds of his office window. "No, it isn't very scientific, but the situation is . . . real. She's a smart woman, our Eleanor. And she likes to get her way, she does. Sometimes she won't let a body rest . . . until she gets her way."

He turns back toward me, shakes a confirming finger. "No matter what you see, no matter how she acts with you, you must see through the carefully constructed facade, the rhymes and reasoning of her game. The woman wants help-I sincerely believe that. And I believe she's waiting here for it."

"Then give it to her. And get her out of here."

Doctor Andy sits resigningly. "That's your job."

"How do you know that?"

"In her own way, she let me know."

"How? When?"

"In . . . the dreams."

We stare silently at each other, both feeling helpless. A moment, then a pudgy finger reaches out, presses an intercom switch.

"Yes, Doctor."

"Harriet, could you come in here, please?"

The office door quickly opens; a pleasant-looking, middle-aged black woman frames the doorway.

"Harriet, Mister MacKenzie would like to see Ms. Pepper. He'll be out in a moment."

Harriet smiles and heads out as I stand to go. I pause. "Tell me, Doctor. Are you still having . . . uncommon dreams?"

"No. They stopped a few nights ago. When I agreed to let Eleanor check-in." The cap is unscrewed, the bottle poured. "Probably about the same time you suddenly decided to visit our fair hinterland."

I turn to go.

"Oh. Guy."

I look back; Doctor Andy is steadily holding the filled shot glass before him. "In my last dream, she said . . . it's coming."

I shrug my shoulders. "Well, I'm here now, aren't I?"

Vodka spills as Doctor Andy's hand begins to shake anew. "I don't think she was referring to you."

9

With a friendly, trusting air, Harriet walks me through twisting, linoleum tile corridors, awash with the smell of institutional astringent and emptiness.

"Doctor Andy really isn't that bad a guy, you know," she states protectively.

I decide that honesty is probably the best policy. "Harriet, how can the guy run even an emptying sanatorium with his drinking problem?"

Harriet lightly touches my arm, guiding me leftward down an intersecting corridor. "Andy doesn't run this place, Guy. He's just a staff doctor, holdin' the line while the Director and most everyone else is settlin'-in at the new facility. As for Andy's hittin' the bottle"-we halt before a metal room door. Harriet points with her thumb "-his sauce problem was back under control, until Little Miss Rock 'N Roll showed up, here."

Harriet produces a jangle of keys on a large metal ring and begins working on a bar lock. I notice that someone has scrawled a room number across the door in blue magic marker. Harriet pauses with her hand on the lock handle and looks at me with genuine concern.

"Look, Guy . . . what has Andy told you about her?"

"Not much, other than Eleanor wanting to be here."

Harriet takes quick measure of me, seems to find what she's looking for and makes her decision. "Okay, couple'a important points you should know, goin' into this."

From a skirt pocket, Harriet produces a pack of cigarettes and a Bic lighter, quickly lights-up. "First off, Little Miss Rock 'N Roll's got Andy spooked out of his mind. I may be just his clerical assistant, but I know when somethin' around here ain't strictly kosher, psychologically-speakin'."

"What do you think's wrong?"

"What I think is wrong is Little Miss Rock 'N Roll checkin' herself in here. What I know is wrong is the set-up."

"The set-up?"

Harriet gestures doorward. "In there. I ain't seen nothin' like it since the bad old days around here, in the late-sixties. Just re-member-this ain't Andy's fault. She insisted on the set-up in there, if you can believe it."

I stand silent, patiently waiting on Harriet's next point.

"Second, you got three days-includin' today-to save my bosses' fat butt."

"Come again?"

"Little Miss Rock 'N Roll's admission is illegal. Only the Sana-torium Director can sign-off on a final admission. Like I said, Andy's just a junior staff physician left to watch a couple'a hard cases that ain't been transferred, yet. The Director's comin' back for the final close-out on Thursday."

Harriet nervously flicks cigarette ash. "He comes back and she's still here, Andy's dead-professionally speakin', of course."

"One question, Harriet."

"Shoot."

"Why do you keep calling Eleanor 'Little Miss Rock 'N Roll?"

Harriet grins broadly. "You ain't from around here, huh?"

"No-I'm from back east."

"You ain't never heard of 'Clive Davis,' Guy?"

"The record biz honcho?"

Harriet laughs. "That Eleanor's sharp, she picked it for name recognition, that's for sure! I'm talkin' Clive Davis, the Indy rock band." Harriet points her cigarette at the door. "Little Miss Rock 'N Roll's the lead singer. At least, 'til she showed up here. The group's got potential, for sure. Could be the next Johnny And The Leisure Suits.'"

"Johnny and who?"

Harriet laughs again. "Big Midwestern band. They haven't broke national, yet.Just remember-" Harriet reaches for the door lock handle and yanks "-you got three days, my friend, to wrap-up whatever this is all about. Or else Little Miss Rock 'N Roll and Andy are in a load of deep legal shit." The sound of the bar lock sliding echoes down the empty corridor.

Harriet eyes me like I belong in Byzantium on a more than visiting basis. Then she opens the door.

10

The glare of a naked lightbulb, starkly illuminating bare white walls of emptiness.

A bare mattress abutting one wall, beneath a window candy-stripped with thick black bars. A wooden orange crate filled with record albums on the floor next to the mattress.

Eleanor atop the mattress. With the exception of her stone-washed jeans, her attire is decidedly unfashionable. I highly doubt that the latest haute couture rage in Indiana this summer is the classic-cut straight jacket.

Three sharp, simultaneous impressions that overlap into a three-dimensional portrait of despair: title if *Figure Of A Woman Wrestling With Her Inner Self.*

For Eleanor is indeed literally wrestling with herself. Lying on her side with her back toward the door, she rocks back and forth; a gain of momentum and she flips her constrained torso sideways, rights with a dull thump, legs splayed-out forward, her upper back resting against the wall. With a push of sneakered heels and more side-to-side rocking, Eleanor concentrates on pushing herself toward a more upright seated position.

Standing in the doorway with harriet, I watch the face from my dream as Eleanor performs her inchworm ritual; head slightly bent forward, the tip of her tongue peeking outside the corner of her mouth in studied concentration. That pseudo-Lili face, same Pepper cheekbones and blue eyes, framed by mid-length blonde hair tossled about in search of hands that could provide a needed wash and brushing.

Harriet clears her throat. Eleanor ceases her struggle and looks up. Our eyes lock. Then a manic twinkle illuminates her face, accompanied by a wide, luminous grin.

I recognize an actress putting on a stage face when I see one. Eleanor's one-woman passion play is about to begin. Whether the plot is rooted in comedy, tragedy or a fair mix of both has yet to be determined: I enter, stage forward.

"Welcome *back*, my friends, to the show that *never* ends! Ladies and gentlemen-Emerson, Lake and Palmer!" Eleanor shouts.

I turn and look at Harriet, leaning comfortably in the doorframe. She raises her eyebrows at me in amusement, blows a fine stream of cigarette smoke toward the ceiling. Harriet beckons beyond my shoulder at Eleanor.

"How we doin' over there this mornin', Sweetie?"

"My name isn't Sweetie." Eleanor's manic aura extinguishes itself, her voice sounding dry and tired.

Harriet calls back. "What should I call you, Sweetie?"

Eleanor's face suddenly twists in anger. She sings, her voice filled with sarcasm. "I can call you Betty . . . and Betty if you want to, you can call me Al."

Harriet laughs. "Like I said, don't let it get to you, Guy! Well. I think I'll leave you two lovebirds alone for awhile." The door slams behind me, Harriet's footsteps echoing away.

With Harriet gone, Eleanor relaxes. She looks at me with bright eyes. "Heidy-Ho, Boogie Boy!"

"Don't call me that, little girl."

Eleanor laughs. "I think it suits you well; the lead singer's name from one of my favorite New Wave bands. We are not men, we are Devo!" She shifts to a mask of feigned sweet innocence. "So. Guy MacKenzie. What brings you to our fair metropolis on this lovely summer day?"

I move forward and squat in front of Eleanor. "Sweet dreams and sour nightmares bring me here, Eleanor."

Eleanor's eyes flash apprehensively as she averts her face sideways. Following her gaze, I stand and walk over to the record crate.

"Harriet tells me you sing with your own band."

"It's gone well. We're one of the better Indy groups."

I flip albums in a steady rhythm. "Is that all you do, Eleanor?"

"What the hell do you mean by that?"

"Well, I mean . . . we did a little bit of everything, back in London. Singing, dancing, the works. It all added-up to paying the bills, and you never knew which direction one talent might take you."

She inches up straighter, eyes me coldly. "My bills are working out just fine, thank you. You're the dancing Boogie Boy. I'll stick to singing."

"Still, an acting lesson couldn't hurt your resume. I've got an old stage friend in Muncie who gives lessons-"

"Well, I'm *sure* that I could be a movie star, if I could get out of this place."

I shrug my shoulders. "Hey it's just a suggestion. It's your life." I find the *Pretenders* album near the back of the crate. "Hey Ellie, remember this one?"

I abandon the crate and sit cross-legged on the floor before Eleanor's wrapped figure. Filling with fond remembrance, I scan the fading autograph on the back jacket cover. Eleanor closes her eyes and leans her head back as I read it out loud. "To my best friend's sister Ellie. Happy Birthday, Chili Pepper! Love, Chrissie Hynde."

I smile mistily. "I remember tossing this in the overseas mail for you, one hot August afternoon."

Eyes still closed, Eleanor softly taps her head back against the wall, in tune to some internal beat.

I sit up cross-legged, hold the album in front of me. "It's funny, seeing these records here. No one listens to albums, anymore. It's all CD's and some cassettes. You go into even most second-hand music stores today, most of them don't even carry real records."

"Vinyl is over, baby." Tap. Tap. Tap.

"Yeah, but you still have your old records, Ellie. They go where you go. Most people carry the past around with them in their heads. You carry your past around with you in an old orange crate."

I move closer, hold up the album jacket. "Like the song says-'I went back to Ohio . . . my city was gone . . . I was stunned and amazed . . . my childhood memories . . . ' Chrissie went home searching for her past and found it all erased. You're lucky enough to have yours here in this box-this city-and yet you're intent as all hell on erasing it. Forgetting it." I move closer. "Threatening to make us forget it."

Eleanor stops tapping. Her eyes flash open, fixing me with twin beacons of smug sky blue. "Sorry, Boogie Boy. You're gonna have to do better than that to save the world."

"You mean your world."

"I mean our world. Our memories. You. Me. Mother and Dad."

A sudden chill runs through me. I stand. "I came to help. But if need be, I'll fight you to the bone, Kid Sister. I went through too much awhile ago to lose Lili again. *I'll never forget.*"

Eleanor smiles her sweet stage smile. "Then do something about it. I mean, that's why you're here, isn't it?"

"Eleanor, there's no need for it to be this way. Why do you insist on being in here?"

She looks thoughtful for a moment, then sings seriously. "Right here, right now, there is no other place that I would rather be."

"I'll see you tomorrow, Ellie."

"See you in your dreams, pal."

11

Barbara Anne and I again stand side-by-side at the kitchen sink, she washing and rinsing, I drying and stacking.

By the time I am finished telling her about my encounter, the last, few unwashed dishes have been abandoned; Barbara Anne stares down into the dark water. She speaks softly, almost a husky whisper. "It's probably not natural to you, you know." She looks up sadly. "You've probably picked it up from Lili, if that's possible. What do you think?"

I pause in wiping a stray dish:

It is a very early morning in London. I feel the heat of the dying hearth fire slowly drying my body as I lay entwined with Lili. She takes my face in her slick hands, gazes at me eye-to-eye, slight inches apart. It is there for only an instant. In the merest of microseconds, for the first and last time ever, raw, unadulterated fear pours from Lili's sweet eyes into my own. The power of her emotion burns into the core of my brain, spreading bright spots to flicker and dance about my vision. Then it is all gone, and all that I perceive is myself reflected in my sated lover's vision.

"Guy?" Barbara Anne's voice faintly echoes from far away.

It is later in the London day. I take the Thesaurus off of our apartment shelf, thumb through it in search of a description of Lili's look, when she held my face in her wet hands. I finally find a word that fits it best:

Premonitory.

"Guy, are you all right?"

"Barbara Anne, what's happening to all of us?"

She gives me a slight, reassuring smile and beckons me to sit with her at the kitchen table. "My mother used to call it 'our special forgetting.' I don't know how long it's been in the women of my family."

Barbara Anne neatly folds her hands before her and watches them as she continues. "It's an avoidance mechanism, I say. A sudden juncture in a life when one cannot avoid having to face one's own overwhelming feelings of grief and loss. So one's mind somehow reaches out and works to make the painful memories go away from those we have to face . . . the letters and mementos that hold memory go away, too."

"It's happened to you?"

She nods, still watching her hands. "One night I spoke to my mother in her dream. But my mother knew. The way of it had been handed down, mother to daughter. We faced the pain together. We got through it."

I stand up. "This is different. Nothing's really missing, is there? And you, me and Cecil-we remember our Lili. So far, Eleanor has only threatened to make us forget."

"She's stronger than I was when it happened to me, Guy. Part of her is trying to fight it off." Barbara Anne's brow furrows. "But something is gone. Last week . . . it's just on the tip of my mind . . . but I can't remember."

I move toward her and place a reassuring hand on her sagging shoulder. "*Think,* Barbara Anne," I urge. "What did Eleanor make you forget? What's missing? Lili died thirteen years ago . . . what is triggering this to happen, now?"

"I don't know . . . for some reason, you're the key." She looks up pleadingly. "She doesn't want to face it, but knows she has to . . . and I'm not the one who can help her." Barbara Anne's wide eyes fill, her voice breaking. "Help her, Guy. Bring our girl back." She tries to smile through her tears. "Don't be afraid to dream, Guy."

The evening sleep is slow to come.

I am again immobile on my back. Eleanor is already in the bedroom, the door closed behind her. We are again both naked, my resultant feeling a mixture of embarrassment and obvious arousal.

As if reading my thought, Eleanor laughs. She langorously rubs her thumb about her left nipple, seductively licks her lips. "Funny things about dreams, Guy. You just can't help but be . . . totally exposed to the other person. Know what I mean?"

I struggle to reply but no sound comes out. Eleanor grins smugly. "Oh, I'm so sorry, Guy. I'm just not in the mood to listen to you right now."

She arches her back, raising her left hand above her head. "A little mood music, if you please." Her raised fingers snap once, loudly; the air fills with the steady, hypnotic sound of Eric Burden crooning "Spill The Wine."

Eleanor's nude form sways to the beat as she moves to stand over me. With a wink and a leer she crawls onto the bed, swings one leg over and straddles me on her knees. She stretches down atop me, elbows rubbing against my arms, eyes burning lustfully an inch from my own. Eleanor's warm brushing breath and soft skin raise the sound of my heartbeat in my ears, her own heart joining the pace.

A small, husky chuckle rumbles from her throat. "Dig if you will the picture . . . of you and me engaged in a kiss." Eleanor's eyes close as she moves forward. Her deep kiss slowly enters me, meeting my resistance, beginning to push it backward. Terror rises within as I fight to hold the emotional line, inwardly struggle to grasp a semblance of token control.

She breaks the kiss and gazes at me with a caring look, stroking my cheeks with both hands. "Relax, Guy. I may not be her, but . . . " she sings softly " . . . if you can't be with the one you love, honey, love the one you're with."

Light fingertips run along my immobile arms, restoring control. "A little free will, for being such a good kisser." She turns her head appraisingly, watches me with raised eyebrows. "Do you *really* want to wake up right now, Guy?" She leans in for another kiss.

The last thread of resistance snaps as I encircle my arms about Eleanor. Raising her face, she gives forth a deep, triumphant laugh as my lips find her neck. "That's a *good* Boogie Boy!"

Eleanor sits back to watch me with amusement as I breathe raggedly, struggling to speak. "Not yet, my sweet Guy-all in good time." A finger runs down my chest. "Know what, Guy?"

My eyes ask.

Her finger finishes its journey downward, hand disappearing between us. Eleanor's breathing rapidly increases. "I want you . . . I don't want anybody else . . . and when I think about you, I *touch* myself."

With a short cry, Eleanor leans forward anew and kisses me deep, then quickly breaks off. She reaches back to grasp my erection, grins as I start. "Pretty little thing, let me light your chemicals," she whispers, then eases backward onto me.

Afterward, Eleanor rests astride me, her ear pressed against my chest listening to my steady heartbeat beneath her own. She sighs deeply, warm breath tickling my throat. "Two strings . . . two strings beating in sympathy." Her hand moves upward, fingers lightly caressing my lips. "Penny for your thoughts, Boogie Boy."

I lightly kiss the top of Eleanor's head. "You make the dead men come."

Eleanor laughs with delight. "Good choice, Boogie Boy!" She runs her fingernails about my chest.

There is a light knocking at the bedroom door.

Eleanor's head snaps up with raccoon alertness. She glares at me fiercely. "What the hell was that?"

The knocking repeats.

"What the fuck are you doing?" she whispers, apprehension rising in her eyes.

I smile a sweet stage smile. "Why don't we ask and find out . . . who's come knocking at my door?"

Twin daggers of sky blue glare at me as I take a deep breath. I turn my head to call out.

"No!" Eleanor whispers fiercely, cupping her hand over my mouth. I grin against her palm, eyes daring her.

She removes her hand and turns. "Who-who's there?"

Lili's voice echoes through the door. "Ellie, is that you? Is Guy in there?"

Eleanor sits horror struck as I place my lips against her ear and whisper, "it was twenty years ago today, Sargent Pepper taught the band to play."

The doorknob begins to turn.

With a terrified scream, Eleanor turns and flings herself at me, attacks with a manic flurry of punches, slaps and scratching fingers. I am again helplessly silent and immobile, my vision blocked by Eleanor's full body barrage.

We both hear the sound of the door creaking open. Eleanor screams anew, clutches my throat with both hands and painfully presses her thumbs downward. I struggle to breathe.

"Ellie?" Lili's voice. Neat the door, questioning.

"No-o-o!" Eleanor wails.

Eyes bulging in animal terror, she puts real body weight into it, pressing her thumbs even harder. Spots dance in my vision, painting out Eleanor's face.

"Make it stop! *Now!*" Eleanor shrills.

From a distant point, I hear the reed-like sound of my windpipe snapping. I have one final, frantic thought:

Sour nightmares.

I awaken with an aching lower back and a very sore throat. Downstairs, I find Cecil and Barbara Anne just leaving for the State Fair. Barbara Anne lingers with me at the kitchen table. She holds her purse in her lap, eyeing me hopefully. "Did you dream last night?"

I spoon honey onto toast in an effort to ease my raging throat. "How was it?"

I swallow with difficulty. "It was . . . educative."

"In what way?"

I absently pick at stray toast crumbs with sticky fingers. "I learned that the old wives' tale is wrong. You do awaken after dying in a dream."

12

On the ride into the city I stop at the Seven-Eleven on West Ra-
vine and purchase a roll of Hall's menthol-eucalyptus throat loz-
enges. The Pakistani store clerk greets me in lilting accent like an
old, familiar friend. He solemnly places my coined change one by
one in my outstretched palm, nods at me supportively. "You have
a very productive day now."

"I'll do my best," I assure him.

He nods affirmatively. "In the long run, that is all anyone has
the right to ask of you."

I have always been quick to follow new-found stage direction.
A brisk walk down the halls of Byzantium and I come to the room,
the door ajar.

Inside, Eleanor sits wrapped and cross-legged on her mattress,
head tilted forward. Harriet squats by her side, softly humming as
she runs a brush through washed golden tresses.

"Good morning, ladies."

Harriet looks up with a warm smile. "Good mornin', yourself." Eleanor ignores me as Harriet resumes her brushing. "I just
thought it would be nice for Eleanor to look clean and fresh for her
guest, today. The night staff tells me we had a bad nightmare in
here, last night."

I move forward and stand before the women. "That so, Ellie?"

From beneath shifting hair and moving brush, her lips and
jaw pout; she speaks sulkily. "The wind is in from Africa. Last
night I couldn't sleep."

Harriet shrugs and stands. "Well, I've got real work to do. I'll
leave the both of you to your own devices."

The door closes behind Harriet and Eleanor raises her head. With closed eyes, she begins her incessant head tapping against the wall. The stress lines under her eyes were absent yesterday.

I move over to the orange crate and flip record jackets forward. "Your hair looks nice this morning, Eleanor. You're lucky that Harriet takes the time to come in here and care."

"When you spend time in a city hotel/you can get company by ringing a bell."

"You ever come up with anything original, Ellie?"

She takes a deep breath, sings slowly as she continues tapping:

> "Oh, somewhere there are screamers,
> And somewhere there are not,
> But I am dear to the crazed ones here,
> In life that is my lot."

I keep flipping records, shake my head. "Don't get too comfortable. You can't stay locked in here, forever."

Eleanor stops tapping and opens her eyes, dully watches as I sit back and scan the back of an old Peter & Gordon jacket cover.

"Lock me away, and don't allow the day . . . here inside . . . where I stay with my loneliness."

"Cut the maudlin crap, Ellie. You'd think you have the market cornered on loneliness."

She smiles wearily. "I've certainly got a lead on it, given the name, and all."

"What, is your middle name 'Loneliness,' or something?"

She looks at me, surprised. "Yes, it is."

I stare back, uncomprehending.

She shakes her head, incredulous. "You really don't know?"

"No, I don't."

Red anger rises in her cheeks. She glares at the orange crate, voice tinged with deep-held resentment. "They named me Rigby. Eleanor Rigby Pepper."

I stare dumbfounded. "I can't believe Lili never told me that!"

Eleanor snorts sarcastically. "Barbara Anne gave *her* the more personal middle name, of course. But *me* . . . " she nods at the record crate " . . . you said yesterday that you mailed The Pretenders album to me on an August afternoon. I was born late in the afternoon on August 8, 1966. That morning, 'Eleanor Rigby' was released as a single in the U.S. They heard it on the radio and gave me the name!" She tries to shrug confined shoulders. "But hey, what's really in a name, huh?"

A sudden thought occurs. I rapidly flip through some record albums. "There are no Beatles albums in here, at all."

Eleanor's face twists with contempt. "Damn right, there aren't! It's bad enough to be named after that piece of misery. I don't need to hear any more of their depressing ballads."

Eleanor closes her eyes and begins tapping backwards again. I stand.

"We've danced around her enough, Ellie."

Eleanor squints her eyes shut harder, taps with increasing speed.

"What are you afraid to face, Ellie?" I take a cautious breath. *"What's coming?"*

With a cry of anguish, Eleanor smashes her head back against the wall, the sound richocheting about the room like the echo of a billiard break.

I move quickly and get a hand between the wall and her rebounding head; a shrill cry as Eleanor encounters my real flesh instead of wall.

"You son of a bitch!" She twists her head sideways and snaps teeth at my wrist, grazing it. I instinctively fall back and Eleanor turns with me. We wordlessly roll about the mattress, she trying to bite and kick, I grunting. Blind momentum carries us off the mattress, tumbling us toward the records. Eleanor smacks the back of her head into the orange crate.

Time stands still.

I sit with my back lodged stiffly against the crate, cradling Eleanor in my arms. We both breath down like spent lovers. I absently stroke Eleanor's hair as she lies, her head in my lap, staring wide-eyed at the ceiling.

"That hurt."

"As much as my broken windpipe?" I reach into my pocket and pop myself a throat lozenge. She smiles. I pop one into her mouth too, for good measure. We rest awhile, the bright silence broken by light, teeth-clicking lozenge sounds.

"Please trust yourself, Ellie." I curl a strand of her hair around my finger. "Face Lili with me."

She turns her head away, the strand unraveling.

"I was afraid too, Ellie. Then I faced up to the hurt with a friend in a coffee shop. And one day I realized that people come and people go, but Lili-the good memories of Lili-are always right here with me, inside. I need them."

I absently fumble with a straight jacket buckle, tug fruitlessly at a tight strap. "You need them, too. Don't push her away, Ellie. Don't make us forget."

Eleanor shrugs off of my lap. Lying straight, she rolls away from me, side over side, up and onto the mattress. She bends herself up and sits cross-legged facing the wall, her restrained back to me.

"Guy." Barely a whisper.

I walk over to her, gently place my hands down on her shoulders.

"What you need." She barely indicates her head toward the orange crate. "It's right there at the house . . . in the other collection."

Eleanor slumps her head forward, brow pressing against the bare wall.

I bend forward, softly press my cheek into her hair; two tears drip from my face, merge into a single line along a strand of Eleanor's hair and drip down to a canvas-covered shoulder.

The drop fades into dryness.

13

I have a very restless night. Eleanor does not choose to visit; as a result, I toss and turn fitfully, awakening several times to be groggily surprised at finding the bed empty of some half-expected dream-mate. Shortly after dawn I give up the attempt and head down to the kitchen. Scrounging up some honey, I head for the front porch.

Cecil is seated on the front porch before a small card table, upon which squats a large, bulky-looking short-wave radio. With his ensign's cap buffered by an unwieldy-looking set of earphones, Cecil sits oblivious to the world, beefy hands twisting and turning dials, adjusting and calibrating.

I sit down on the porch swing and steadily work through the honey, watching Cecil mutter and tune in a surprisingly delicate-looking dance of radioscopic surveillance. After awhile Cecil stretches and seeing me, grins and doffs the headpiece; a light static sound faintly purrs from the receptors. Cecil shakes his head in good-natured exasperation. "I never could get this darned thing to work. Though some mornings, I still just can't resist trying."

Cecil walks to the porch rail. Placing both hands on the rail he inhales deeply, his large chest ballooning up and out, eyes shut in early morning farm rapture. A momentary pause and Cecil exhales explosively, then turns to me with a beatific look on his face.

"My God, son, there's nothing on this good green earth like it! The bee-fried air!"

I lick the last bit of honey from my spoon and look at Cecil, puzzled.

"The bee-what?"

Cecil's look turns to one of gentle surprise. "Don't you remember your Bradbury?"

"I'm afraid not."

Cecil sighs and fondly shakes his head. From the card table he picks up a worn paperback, comes over and sits next to me on the porch swing. The book is held with gentle reverence within his large hands; Cecil looks at it and speaks in a soft voice tinged with deep fondness.

"*Dandelion Wine*, Guy. Ray Bradbury's American classic novel of a young Midwestern boy's God-given summer. I reread it every summer. My bible." He looks up at me, his aging eyes beaming with the still-bright light of his faraway youth. "I was born in Waukegan, Illinois on June 7, 1928-Bradbury's hometown, eight years after his own birth. I remember his name from my boyhood.

"The summer of '28's the setting." His voice trails off, finger-tips lightly stroking the worn bookcover. "That's my own boy-hood in there. Like the last page says, summer here in the Mid-west is like a day . . . June dawns, July noons, August evening's over, gone with only the sense of it all left behind.

"So toward the beginning of every July, nearing the high noon of summer's day, I take the book off its shelf and reread a piece of my boyhood . . . say hello to my memories, dip my mind in the cool-watered strength and wisdom of home, have myself a good, long strong fill of dandelion wine."

Cecil looks up and sees the lump in my throat, gazes into my filling eyes with strong fatherly care.

"It's Eleanor, isn't it, son?"

I swallow hard.

"Mother means well, but I know my girl. Both my girls." He places a large hand on my shoulder and holds up the book in the other as I look downward. "There's a place in here where the boy's in trouble. And someone says of him, that 'some people turn sad awfully young.'" He pauses, then continues more quietly. "The summer after Lili died, I thought of that written passage whenever I thought of my little Ellie. They say time heals, but the wound never totally closed for her."

"I want to help her, but I can't figure out how."

"A piece of advice, at least. If there's one thing I've learned in my sixty-three years, it's this-it's the child still within the heart that helps the adult on the surface eventually come to terms with the world and its ways." He opens my hand and places the worn book in it. "Why don't you hang onto this for awhile, do some reading when you get the chance? I've got it all down to memory now, mostly."

Cecil stands and walks back to his radio. "Well, I think I'll give this awhile longer of trying. Then I've got to finish cataloging my video collection before we leave for State Fair."

"A collection you say, Cecil?" I ask, my voice aquiver.

Cecil nods as he turns back to the radio, begins to re-don his headgear.

"Mind if I look through it?"

"Be my guest, son, be my guest," he mumbles, already lost again in his quest through ethereal static.

The clue lies within the most recent tapes.

I begin with Monday, June 17; after hitting PLAY, I begin FAST FORWARD. Ted Koppel, his guests and staffers pantomime across the screen in jerky, Keystone Kop-like spasms. June 18 . . . June 19.

June 20 is gone.

I can just make out a split-second image of Koppel, hear the "Good-" of his June 20 show introduction. Then the tape is blank for a half-hour length. Not the normal static, gray-and-white pixel blank of a new tape or an erasure. Just blank. A pure, silent nothing.

I shut off the VCR and reach for the phone that sits on a nearby desk. The ABC local network affiliate staffer is more than happy to tell me the topic of the June 20 Nightline show. He is especially proud of the local twist to the episode.

I numbly hang-up the phone. Looking up, I find Barbara Anne framing the doorway in morning bathrobe and slippers, hands in her robe pockets. She eyes me curiously.

"Is everything okay, Guy?"

There is only one honest answer.

"It's here."

14

The drive to Byzantium seems to flow along in slow motion.

Down the corridors to face to door. I pause and hear no sound from within. The key fits the lock easily, the lock bar moves smoothly. I open the door.

Eleanor sits cross-legged on her mattress, staring off to the side. She slowly turns her head to gaze at me, eyes ringed with dark circles of sleeplessness.

"You look like you've been up all night, Ellie." I move toward her. "Grab your things. I've come to take you home."

She utters a tension-laced giggle. "Peter Gabriel."

"Enough, already. Puzzle-time is over, Ellie."

I remove the long sheath from its perch in my back pocket and slide out the hunting knife. Eleanor tries to scrabble back farther against the wall, eyes bulging with sudden shock at seeing the lethal-looking, eight-inch blade glinting in the morning light.

"Relax. I'm on your side, remember?"

The blade snicks through the straight jacket strap as if parting a warm stick of butter. Another moment, and the remaining restraints are severed. Eleanor sits dully watching my hands as I work to pull the untied jacket off of her.

Just as the wound jacket comes off, Doctor Andy and Harriet arrive. They stand expectedly, watching as Eleanor absentmindedly tries to smooth-out the wrinkles in her freed white blouse.

"Do you feel steady enough to walk?"

"It's been a few days," Eleanor croaks. "I can try."

I help her struggle up; she leans heavily against me as we move slowly toward the door. Doctor Andy and Harriet follow behind us with the records. Doctor Andy heaves the crate into the Geo

Prizm trunk; he and Harriet offer quick, relieved goodbyes, then dwindle in the rear-view mirror as we leave the sanatorium grounds.

As we drive, Eleanor stares about with a helpless look, nervously twisting and wrapping her seatbelt shoulder strap about her recently-freed hands. "This isn't the way home."

I press down on the gas pedal, pick-up a bit of speed.

"We're going into the city, aren't we?"

"Uh-huh."

Eleanor slumps to her right, head bent forward in despair. "It's here?" she whispers.

"It's here."

I reach over and supportively pat here arm. "With me, it was a letter. With you, it was a VCR tape. When it comes to memory, Ellie, you're high-tech all the way."

The Geo Prizm glides onward down straight, Middle-American streets etched upon the face of this Midwestern city. As we turn onto West 38th Street, I notice an increase of pedestrians in the area.

Eleanor presses her forehead against the passenger window, arms and hands entangled in the seatbelt as a meager pacifier for the security of the abandoned straight jacket. She stares at the passing strollers, begins to softly sing in a rythmic tone, over and over, a personal mantra for protection against the inevitable: "Shiny happy people holding hands, shiny happy people holding hands . . . "

At the 1200 block of West 38th Street I take a left off the roadway. The Geo Prizm enters the elegantly landscaped grounds of the Indianapolis Museum Of Art. We pull up in front of the new Mary Friedrich Hulman Pavilion. "The eagle has landed," I mutter, shutting off the car engine.

I open the passenger door, untangle Eleanor from her seatbelt. She stands and stares numbly at the pavilion entrance. "I don't want to do this."

I take her arm. "Yes, you do. That's why we're here. I've called ahead-they know why we're here."

Arm in arm, we walk slowly up the short steps and inside. We move haltingly down the pavilion main corridor, occasionally passing a visitor to one of the permanent exhibits. Eleanor moves as if in a trance. Old feelings, both good and bad, faintly stir deep within me.

We reach the rear of the pavilion corridor, the entrance to tomorrow's opening show. The area is quiet and deserted; the curator has had the decent discretion to unlock the door and retreat to a distance.

Eleanor and I stop and stare at the exhibit sign. Soft light emanates from within the room.

"I can't," Eleanor chokes. I catch her as her knees buckle, pick her up in my arms. She feels light and fragile, breathes steadily as she turns her face protectively into my chest.

"Yes, you can," I whisper into her ear. "We can . . . together."

With arms full of Eleanor, I enter into the Robert Mapplethorpe Traveling Retrospective Photography Exhibit.

We move along the Mapplethorpe exhibit walls.

Past the exquisite flowers . . . "Irises" . . . "Double Jack-In-The-Pulpit" . . . "Calla Lily" . . .

Past "Urn With Fruit" . . .

Past the portrait series . . . "Katherine Cebrian" . . . "Francesco Clemente" . . . "Doris Saatchi" . . .

Past the photos of lovers . . . "Embrace" . . . "Thomas and Dovanna" . . .

Past the glassed top display case holding the photographs of sweet children and honest feelings, the images at the focal point of yesterday's and tomorrow's heated controversy . . .

I pause for a moment at "Self-Portrait (1980)."

Then I turn and move on to the final exhibit photograph. It is a distance away from the others, discreetly alone before a small marble museum bench. Halting with my back to the photograph, I place Eleanor down on the bench, face-forward. She clutches her arms across her stomach, stares forlornly at the floor. I sit down next to her.

"No," she whispers.

I take her hand. "You know, Ellie . . . I'll bet that all the power between you and me . . . all the power in the entire world, couldn't make this photograph go away."

She jerks her hand out of mine and turns around on the bench, back to the wall and buries her face in her hands. I stand and walk around to face her.

A moment passes as I watch her, still and helpless as an exhausted, wounded bird.

"Ellie, not all memories are direct. I mean, experiences happen and we remember them. But sometimes other people tell us about their experiences, and the telling is so special, so full of love and meaning for that person, that the told experience becomes a part of the listener. In a way, it becomes our own direct memory.

"I have one of those memories inside me, Ellie. It was told to me by a big sister who was very sick and in a lot of pain, and yet traveled to go home for one brief, final visit . . . to see her little sister for the last time.

"She loved to dance, while her little sister loved to sing. And on that final visit home, the big sister felt strong enough to suggest that the two of them put on a show in the living room for their parents. It had been a small family tradition before the big sister left home to seek her own way on the stage. They spent that last visit together with skits, and jokes, and sing-alongs. For the finale-"

"Stop it," Eleanor whispers. "Sweet dreams and flying machines in pieces on the ground," she sings frantically.

"-the family gathered together," I continue. "Ellie played her guitar, and they all sang Lili's favorite song. Together. A Beatles song."

I sing it softly:

> Blackbird singin' in the dead of night/
> Take these broken wings and learn to fly/
> All your life/

You were only waiting for this moment to be free/
You were only waiting for this moment to be free/
You were only waiting for this moment to be free.

Fingers spread slightly as Eleanor carefully peeks out from behind her hands. I hold my breath, waiting; Eleanor stares at me,
eyes wide and child-like, shaded deep within splayed fingers. Slowly
she turns around on the bench and then stands, hands moving
downward to cover her cheeks and mouth. I come around and
stand behind her, gently place my hands on her shoulders. Together we support each other as we look at it.

The photograph is small, thinly matted and bordered by a
plain frame. Yet the power of it is raw and undeniable, causing the
viewer upon first look to avert one's eyes from the subject's return
gaze, glance downward to the small title card beneath the frame,
focus in brief respite upon the typewritten title letters:

Lilith Anne Pepper: Dying (1978)

On a gray, wet London afternoon she stands alone on a deserted sidewalk-somewhere near Beal Street, I think-dancer's body
wasting away behind thick folds of dark woolen overcoat, chemo-
ravaged hair tucked beneath a matching headscarve. Her face over-
whelms the soul, causes all other elements of the photograph to
fade away like the thinnest of litmus colors. Lili's eyes sit atop
fragile, hollowed cheeks, blazing with the power of twin blue suns
suddenly gone nova; eyes that fill a dying face with a light of in-
tensity and power and understanding and acceptance and stark
serenity. *Here I am,* Lili silently blazes at us, *mine is the candle that
burns shortest but oh, so brightest. Look at me! I have faced it and
walked through it and accepted it and I am utterly fearless and at
peace. And I can give to you because of it. Take strength from me.*

"We didn't know Mapplethorpe," I whisper. "Just passed by
on an afternoon walk. Her saw her and asked, and we said okay.
He said one thing I'll never forget. That when they someday hang

a retrospective of his work, he'll have left instructions for the entire exhibit to be titled by what Lili's photograph meant to him."

One trembling hand leaves Eleanor's cheek, slowly moves toward Lili; fingertips halt just before the glassed photograph cover.

"The Perfect Moment," Eleanor whispers; the sound of it hangs in the air like far-off Fall leaves gingerly breezing along a sidewalk in childhood memory.

Then one finger lightly presses the glass, quickly brushing Lili's cheek. The connection is made. With loud, heaving sobs Eleanor folds into my arms.

There is no need to whisper consoling words. She knows I feel the same.

That is why I am here.

15

Eleanor and I sit in the Geo Prizm in front of the pavilion, the engine softly idling.

"I hated you for so long, Guy."

I look at her in surprise. She stares off across the parking lot. "Lili should have stayed here at home with us, at the end. There wasn't any reason for her to go back to London. Except for you."

"That's not true. If anything, I encouraged her to think about us coming back to Indy for good. But she would have none of it; the West End stage was where Lili came of age as an independent adult and it was there she insisted on dying. She had the right to make that final decision."

I aimlessly run my hands about the steering wheel grip. "She never came out and said it, but . . . I think she loved you and Barbara Anne and Cecil too much to watch you go through the pain of her final days."

Eleanor continues staring off into the landscaped distance. She scratches one hand through her hair and sighs.

"I still feel lost."

I let go of the steering wheel and pick-up Cecil's tattered copy of *Dandelion Wine*. "I felt that way for eleven long, slow years. Then I found out the hard way where the answer was."

Eleanor turns and looks at me quizzically.

I tap my chest. "It's right here. Inside. Think of the good memories of Lili, even some of the bad times, in which at least you were together and depended upon each other, and cared. And you'll feel found. If not for yourself, then do it for Lili. She needs to be remembered by us." I hold up *Dandelion Wine,* steadily riffle the pages from front to back. "Like it says in the book." I hold it out to Eleanor, my finger pointing out the line.

She leans forward and reads it aloud. "No person ever died that had a family." She looks up as I close the book.

"That's us-you, me, Barbara Anne and Cecil."

Strong light shines in Eleanor's eyes. Smiling fondly, she places a hand lightly on my neck and pulls me forward, kisses me softly and brief. Eleanor's gaze dances to my forehead. She reaches up and tugs sharp and quick, holds forth one solitary strand of white.

I laugh. "My first gray hair! This baby boomer's getting old!"

Eleanor smiles. "Or could it be a touch of wisdom."

"That's highly debatable."

Eleanor holds two fingers up to her mouth and blows, the gray strand fluttering over my shoulder and out the window. "Oh well, a touch of gray/kind'a suits you, anyway."

"Ellie, do me a favor. Don't ever quote a song lyric to me ever again, okay?" I shift the Geo Prizm into drive as she tilts her head back and roars a thick husky laugh, a purely Pepper-woman sound.

As we turn out of the museum driveway, I secure my seatbelt. "Aren't you gonna buckle-up, Ellie?"

She glances down, then smiles. "I've been buckled-up enough lately, thank you. I'm willing to take my chances."

I shrug my shoulders. "Hey, it's your life."

She beams. "Ain't it, though?"

EPILOGUE

It is the time of dusk in dandelion wine country. We four have returned from the final day of State Fair, where Cecil's prize hog Big Blue took a ribbon. Eleanor and I sit on the porch swing, watching the sun set, while Cecil is seated before his radio, searching the heavens.

The screen door opens and Barbara Anne steps onto the porch, a deep bowl in each hand; she passes them to Eleanor and me. "Old-fashioned lime-vanilla ice . . . my special recipe.

I dip my spoon and taste. "Hey, this is really something!"

Eleanor swallows and nods in agreement. "I'll say!"

Suddenly, Cecil leaps up, his chair sliding backwards. "Listen!" he cries. His burley arm yanks the headphone jack out of the radio socket; the radio amps fill the early evening air with the sound of Fab Four voices:

> "It's been a hard day's night,
> And I've been workin' like a dog,
> It's been a hard day's night,
> I should be sleepin' like a log,
> But when I get home to you,
> You know the things that you do,
> They make me feel all right.
> You know I feel all right."

Cecil plugs his headphones back in, then sits back down with a deep, contented sigh, closes his eyes to listen.

Eleanor and I look at each other and laugh.

"You don't mind that it was them?"

She smiles. "I don't mind . . . now."

I take her hand in mine. "Once more would be okay," I whisper. "Just for old time's sake."

She smiles as she whispers back. "And in the end, the love you take/is equal to the love you make."

The Bulgarian Poetess Takes A Green Card

"Actuality Is A Running Impoverishment Of Possibility."
THE BULGARIAN POETESS
John Updike (1966)

I always think of Marti as my Bulgarian Poetess. She took the boom tube from the East Bloc colony on Sofia in the Proxima Centauri system into Boston early that fall, as part of the East-West cultural exchange that reared its head during that warming trend in bloc relations.

It was a heady time for me. Barely into my early thirties, at that moment I was the prodigal son of the Harvard-Radcliffe American Studies Department. My star shone at its brightest that season. I had just played out a successful round of Machiavellian pick-up sticks with the boys and girls across the Charles at B.U., was rewarded for my efforts with a multi-world university press printing of my newly-completed, first post-doctoral project.

Late-20th century American fiction was and still is my specialty. Although gifted, I was touched by a wide (yet slowly dwindling) streak of latent youth and pretentiousness. I believed with all my heart that the world was mine to hold in both hands as I saw fit, if only I chose to do so; the success of my project only served to enhance that outlook. "Molly As Icon In The Late-20th Century Speculative Fiction Genre: Molly Millions, Mad Molly Peaches, Moya Molly and Molly Dear-An Historiographical Analysis" was received with open arms and academic awe by the length and breadth of the Harvard Yard community, from young undergrads to old emeriti.

I saw myself as the toast of the Town, the pride of the Hub Of The Universe; I only had eyes for me. A wine and cheese in my honor was scheduled for late Friday afternoon in the department library. Marti and the other visiting cross-cultural literati were invited.

"So . . . *different* for you, Cali, this Molly foolishness, and yet such a *surprisingly* respectful reaction," Moravellov purred lightly over his cocktail. He had cornered me rather firmly near the brie-and-gouda tray for an end-of-the-work-week skirmish. The Old Guard had always warned me about Kashka Moravellov; never let your guard down, boy, against that token cross-cultural with the Harvard tenure.

"Different?" I mumbled around a taste of cracker. "How so, Kashka?"

Moravellov sipped lightly, surveyed me from beneath dark eyelids, smiled thinly. "My dear Cali Catt, you're a short . . . *story* writer, nothing more-" he paused for effect, airily waved a dismissive wrist "-nothing less. And yet you . . . *wander* from your own work, if I may label it thus, *choose* to muse over antique period pieces."

He paused to toy with a stray sliver of gouda on his plate, all so thinly veiled. "It's all so . . . so *academic*, don't you agree?"

I tossed back a feral grin. "It ain't workin', Kahka. This is *my* moment in the sun, the first of many, and try as you might you can't rain on it." I drained my wine glass, placed it upside down on the plate he held, smiled sweetly as he glowered.

Our attention was diverted across the room as the library doors swept open, the conversational background hum gearing up an extra notch as a flash of cross-culturals glided into the throng. Marti shone like a flaxen-maned beacon among them.

I had never seen her before then, having had no contact with the current visiting legation. The opposite was true for Moravellov, given his role as cultural exchange officer within the department. His demeanor shifted as he called out in Bulgarian, beckoned Marti to join us.

She was a tall woman, her soft lovely cheeks framed by gentle curves of straw hair, all topped by a fashionable black Eastern hat. Pseudo-military style was the female fashion on Sofia that fall and she wore it well in all-black, her shoulders topped by glittering gold epaulets; a neo-punk Ninotchka adorned in ebony and glitter. Yet her face belied the pseudo-stern fashion, rendering the clothing effect harmless, softening it. Her large, gray eyes, inquisitive, laughed aloud both at and along with the world, drank in everything and everyone about her. They beckoned one to smile back, reach out to greet her, get to know her. The hub of my universe gently slid out from beneath my own feet, softly settled near hers.

"My dear Martina, may I present our most talented junior faculty member, our dear Cali Catt! Under my close tutelage, Cali has only just embarked upon a fiction-writing career which may possibly even surpass this old expatriot's meager yet well-intentioned work!" When it came to bullshitting the tourists for the sake of the Old Towne Team, Moravellov was second to none, ninja faculty politics aside.

Marti surveyed me with smiling eyes. "*Pliss*, call me Marti, Cali." Her voice was strong, laced with both accent and a light honey of raspiness, resonating with a firm assurance. We chatted academically for awhile with Kashka as self-appointed overseer, conversationally offering Marti details of my work, informing me of her renowned poetry.

I was momentarily taken aback. "I was not aware that you are *the* Sofian Martina," I stammered.

"Marti," she corrected.

"Yes . . . Marti." I tasted the name. "Your poetry is so layered, so mature; upon reading "The Checkist Of Alpha Prime" one finds it difficult to picture you as being my age. I've always pictured an older Martina, sort of a female version of Kashka."

She laughed deep and strong, a purely happy sound. I loved her for that laugh. Even Moravellov was forced to accept the barb and join in. "It is a . . . *shame* that Sofian society does not allow surnames, specially regretful for poets," Kashka purred. "Your poetry's uniqueness deserves . . . *personal* recognition."

Marti laughed anew. "The satisfaction of the poem, the being of it, is all that one should require. Within my family my name is unique and recognizable enough, often to their regret."

"How so?" I asked.

"I was raised to be the ninth generation Janet of my family; upon coming of age, I changed my name to Martina." She lightly sipped wine, continued. "I needed an outlet for individuality, as a starting base for my work-I am told that the fifth generation Janet legally changed her name to Humphrey for a day, then changed her mind and reverted." She sipped the last of her wine, lightly held the vacant glass stem sideways. "But then, she was not a poetess, was she?"

She strongly led me in laughter, as Moravellov was collared away by a passing trio of graduate students.

Marti crossed her arms as she gazed down at the rug between us, left foot rubbing languidly across it, back and forth.

"So," she said softly, knowingly. "You're stories? Are they difficult?"

She looked up as we both burst anew into laughter.

"Your Updike," I laughed back. "Is it quotable?"

"I too enjoy last century's late-period American culture," she smiled. "Updike's 'Bulgarian Poetess' . . . it is how I feel inside when the writing is difficult."

"The days that go down like mud."

Marti didn't reply, yet her eyes nodded agreement once, down to the rug and back to my face.

"So, how much longer is your stay here in Boston, Marti?"

"Only until tomorrow evening."

My heart swiftly sank.

"Then the legation moves on to visit universities in eight more North American cities, before boom tubing home, from New Orleans." She grinned mischievously. "The sixth generation Janet in my family had a Bulgarian cousin who immigrated to that city. Do you think that I will be welcomed with open arms in *Nah' Leens?*"

Even with the ache I had to laugh at her southern accent attempt. Yet she saw my heart in my mouth-it flashed as a reflection in her sweet gray eyes.

"So . . . " she trailed off with a soft sigh, gazing about the room. I suddenly noticed that evening was beginning to darken through the library windows; the library now echoed with the clinking of empty wine glasses and abandoned cutlery as a few waitresses gathered up the remnants of the fading gathering.

Marti brightened as she touched my arm. "So . . . Cali Catt."

"Cali," I corrected.

"Yes, like on Sofia." Her fingertips halted at my elbow. "I have read of Updike's Boston. Tell me. Cali's Boston . . . what is it like?"

I showed her Cali's Boston. We monorailed out of Cambridge across the Charles beneath crisp October moonlight, toward downtown steel and glass spires clustered behind bands of squat neighborhoods, winking night reflections in greeting. The city's scale had hardly changed in the century since the days of Updike, yet its flavor had perceptibly altered with the dual flow of time and events; Boston's body wore its cultural clothing in the brightest colorful cuts of late-21st century style.

The city was and always will be the most walkable of urban settings. We alighted from the monorail at Charles Street station, took off on foot into the narrow brownstone neighborhoods of Beacon Hill. The red-bricked townhouses along narrow colonial lanes had blossomed over the preceding years with the flower of renovation, fueled by the latest swirling ripples of ethnicity to wash over the Brahmin hillside. Marti and I walked the Budayeen streets of this Arabic-tinged neighborhood, past gold and turquoise minarets grafted atop refurbished brownstones. "Like turbans worn by proper Yankee tourists," Marti murmured, shifting her grip on my arm.

We wound our way out of the quiet Budayeen streets toward downtown, were swept up by the Salsa beat of State Street, Tremont and Downtown Crossing, the nightlife of the Cuban District.

The evening street festival was reaching fever pitch as Marti and I swam into it, were swept down crowded lanes bursting with neon carnival. We hit all the open air street cafes and banana bars, sipped nutmeg-laced draughts of Coco-Ribe from china blue porcelain shot glasses.

The coconut rum set Marti's eyes afire as we street-danced along with hundreds throughout the District blocks; at some point

we tapered off from the gaiety, gathered breath along a more se-
date, empty length of State Street. We paused beneath a weathered, wrought-iron street lamp, gazed silently at each other; Marti's
face was glistening with the sweat of happiness, her left hand running languidly back through her hair, gray eyes slightly watering,
waiting expectedly. I kissed her slowly, tasted her sweetly; her essence was of Coco-Ribe, warmth and goodness.

"Show me more," she whispered. "Show me the part of the
city that is leaving you."

Hand-in-hand we crossed eastward through downtown, reaching the lip of the city, touched upon the steadily sinking edges of
the waterfront. We crossed walkways straddled above old colonial
lanes now metamorphosized into emerald canals, an aquatic neck-
lace tightening itself around the city's neck.

"I now know what it must have been like to live in Venice
before it submerged," I mused.

Marti's thumb gently caressed the hollow between my thumb
and forefinger. "I wonder which cities will be seen as the Venices
and Bostons of the next century?"

We aimlessly wandered into the outdoor aquarium surround-
ing the elevated Fanueil Hall; with a sudden cry of excitement,
Marti tugged me to the edge of a racing canal-the heated waters
before us were alive with round bursts of bewhiskered racers. In a
flurry of arm-waving and shouting she bet heavily on the seals, was
ahead for awhile then lost big; with a bemused shrug she unfas-
tened the gold epaulet atop her left shoulder, tossing it along with
a shout to the croupier across the canal as a final bet. My protesta-
tions were muted by a nodding smile from Marti, eyes half-lid-
ded, radiating a soft, blissful contentment. "Just wait . . . just wait,"
she murmured. It was over quickly, her seal passed at the finish by
an arrogant-looking pup.

"I'll go trade some cash for the epaulet," I said, turning toward the canal crossover.

"Oh, no," protested Marti. She pulled me in the opposite
direction. "You must *not*, it would be bad luck to retrieve an item

lost on a bet! Sofian custom dictates it as a kind of good luck to chance an epaulet on a spontaneous bet and lose."

"That makes no sense, here," I laughed.

"Oh, it doesn't, does it?" She eyed me, amused. "Have you never seen any of your old American movies, in which a toast is made upon which fine crystal glasses are shattered into a fireplace in celebration?" She again brushed her hand back through her hair. "It is an inexplicable twist of human nature, to often mark celebration with a ceremonial gesture of loss. There is a native Sofian saying that sums up the concept."

"What might that be?"

Marti gazed at me solemnly. "Oob la di, oob la da, life goes on, bra . . . la la-la la, life goes on . . . it would take awhile to explain its full meaning, but-"

She started as I doubled over in hard laughter, tears running down my cheeks. Between gasps, I managed to explain the saying's Earth-bound, Liverpool origins in late-20th century rock 'n roll.

Marti was miffed. "*Well*, at least we on Sofia have kept the old song alive as part of everyday life."

"I'll give you that," I chuckled, wiping away tears of laughter with my palms. "I only know it because of my research."

As we headed back into the Salsa streets, conversation turned toward a shared pleasure of 20th century movie musicals. Fueled anew by more Coco-Ribe, we sang and danced to bits of half-remembered numbers; at the corner of Tremont and School Streets I sat on the curb and gazed in complete admiration as Marti expertly sang and danced her way through her favorite musical number, jumping up and off of the corner wrought-iron street lamp base several times. I stood just as she finished, whirling around and into my arms.

"That was *wonderful!*" I gushed. "How did you remember the whole thing . . . those moves?"

She kissed me quickly, explained as she took my hand and pulled me down Tremont, along the edge of Boston Common. "It is my *favorite*-whenever it is shown back home, I drop whatever I am doing and sit down to see it!"

We skirted the edge of the Common; on the Boylston Street side we halted, Marti gazing into the park. "What is *that*, in there?"

I waved it off. "Oh, it's just an old colonial-era graveyard section of the Common-the city restored it way back when, put up some historical markers."

She pulled me anew. "Come, let us look!"

I held my ground, gazing uneasily into the dark greenery. "I don't know, it might not be too safe in there, this time of night."

Marti pulled harder, excited. "Cali! It is only a few feet into the park! If an urban terrorist grabs you, I will *scream* for help! Besides, there is an Earth saying to cover this situation . . . you only spit once!"

I gave in with another burst of laughter. "That's only *live* once!" I gasped.

The grave area *was* only several yards into the Common, hardly outside of the street light. It had a quieting effect upon us both; the granite markers huddled together on a small hillock buttressed up from the Common by an ivory-colored retaining wall. Marti's breathing steadied as she gazed reverently at the markers, lettering weathered and faded with time. "We must cremate on Sofia," she said softly. "The planet is not kind for proper burial."

She pointed at the markers, mesmerized. "To see the names and to know that they are resting here . . . and yet, the ache of it."

"How so, the ache?" I whispered, gazing with her.

"We know *of* them," Marti replied, "but not *who* each of them was-their lives, their loves, their hopes and fears." Her voice strained. "It is like that poetic line from that old movie . . . all those memories . . . lost in time . . . like tears in rain."

I held my sweet poetess as her own tears ran, gently kissed salty droplets as they slowly arced down her cheeks.

A slight rustling sound hinted behind me. "Cali . . . look," Marti whispered. I turned, eyes focusing in the moonlight; in a bed of leaves between markers a small night rabbit huddled, staring straight at us.

"Make wishes, Cali."

"Wishes?"

"Yes, wishes! Hurry, before it goes away . . . we see few animals on Sofia, it is good luck to make wishes when you see one."

Her arms encircled my waist, pulling me closer, inviting. "Make wishes."

I stroked her cheek, softly kissed her lips between wishes. "I wish I could spend time with you . . . I wish I could talk to you about how I feel about you and how you feel about me . . . I wish I could share so many experiences with you . . . I wish I could make love with you . . . I wish I could just hold you . . . I wish I could just hold your hand . . . I wish a million things . . . All you."

At 3:00 a.m. We walked into The Parker House hotel lobby. Marti typed us into the the check-in computer register as Dr. and Mrs. Desmond and Molly Jones.

3:00 p.m. . . . 3:00 p.m. . . . 3:00p.m. . . . I swatted away at the nightstand, eyes shut, fumbling without success in search of the wake-up box. The time call continued. Reality began to seep in along with the realization that a wake-up ear plug was intoning the moment into my left ear. I sat up, de-plugged and gazed about the bedroom, eventually resting my eyes on Marti. She was sound asleep on her stomach, sheets tangled about her waist, arms wrapped around a pillow, face away from me. I leaned over and lightly rested my cheek in the hollow of her smooth back, felt her breath rythmically rising and falling. A sudden thought occurred.

I gathered clothing and crept out into the sitting room to dress, then headed into the lobby and out into the bright late afternoon sunshine of State Street. The little shop was only two doors down and across the street from The Parker House; I needn't have fully dressed to bop across the way to *Empathy Fred's*, although Freddie wouldn't have been too thrilled. He kept the gift shop all quaint and New Englandy, small display windows crisscrossed with a lace of wooden panes, and an old-fashioned, brass knobbed door that tinkled a bell-chime of greeting when I entered. Freddie was behind the counter whispering to an inventory pc; he looked up, inhaled deeply and tilted his head in thought.

"Let's see . . . a sour smell of stale Coco-Ribe, he looks like something the cat (no pun intended) dragged in, yet his facial expression emotes pure contentment. So . . . this is love."

"Spare it, Freddie," I coughed, walking past him toward the larger back room. "Or I'll flunk your kid this semester-again."

Freddie chuckled following me into the room. "You looking for anything in particular, Cali?"

"I saw an antique card in here, last year-if you still have it, I really want to give it to someone special."

Freddie brightened as he waddled around me to the card rack-cards were his personal favorite stock. He began to randomly heft cards from the rack, open them and gently line them up on an antique mahogany table. A tiny mixture of song began to rise in the room.

"This the one?" *Getting to know you, getting to know all about you; getting to like you, getting to hope you like me . . . "*

"Nope."

"How's about this?" . . . *put a little love in your heart, and the world will be a better place . . .*

"Uh, uh-"

"Ah, hah! This has *got* to be your special one!" We both stared blankly as the card played out.

"You better fix that stutter, Fred, if you ever expect it to sell."

Freddie tinkered with the card as I stooped, perused the bottom row of the rack. "Here it is!" I exclaimed. "I recognize this scratch on the cover!" I straightened, holding the card in both hands.

Freddie glanced up. "You like that one, huh?"

"A friend does-and so do I. How much do I owe you?"

Her eyed me seriously. "This friend must be special, for that card."

I nodded once, bit my lower lip.

"Tell you what, Cali, you get my kid up to a 'C' this term and we'll call it even."

"I really appreciate this, Fred," I said, heading for the street.

"Remember, Doctor Catt, a 'C'! Or I show up to repossess!"

"Have a nice trip to Sofia, Fred," I called back.

Marti was just beginning to rustle awake when I returned. I sat on the edge of the bed, lightly stroked her hair; she looked up and sleepily smiled, stretched, then invitingly held out her arms to me. Sometime later we showered and dressed, then I took her hand and led her into the sitting room.

"So where is this surprise, Cali?"

We sat on the sofa, the unopened card on the low coffee table before us.

"Do you know what this is?" I asked.

"I have no idea."

Silently I reached for the mahogany box, unlatched it and pried open the two sides halfway. The mechanism embedded in the holo-card softly sighed as it emitted a wide circle of light onto the table before us. A six-inch high, wrought-iron streetlamp flickered into existence, streaks of holographic rain fluttering downward through the sepia image. A tiny figure of a man wound one arm and leg around the streetlamp, perching just above the base; Gene Kelly grinned at Marti, swung once around the lamp base then bounded down and into "Singin' In The Rain."

I watched Marti as she stared transfixed by the holo-card, eyes round, the back of her left hand touching her mouth. Gene Kelly finally twirled his umbrella one last time, waved at Marti and ambled through the tapering droplets back into the holo-card. I closed the card and turned back to her.

"Do you like it?"

Her eyes filled as she squeezed my hand tightly. "So beautiful . . . it is my favorite song. Oh, Cali!"

I held her tight. "I hoped you'd like it. They had a George

Harrison singing "My Sweet Lord" but it stuttered, and I know what 'Singin' In The Rain means to you-to us."

Marti sat back and gazed at me softly, hands in mine. "It means so much to me, Cali. I will treasure it-and you-always."

"Stay here in Boston with me, Marti. I love you so much."

She let go of my hands and placed the holo-card in her lap, hands folded atop it. "Sofia is home. A visit to North American Earth on a green card was supposed to be just nice, and has become so special. Yet I cannot live my life, here."

"Then I'll come to Sofia. The university will help-we can be together."

Her fingers fiddled nervously with the latch on the holo-card. "Cali, yesterday afternoon you remarked surprise that I was so young for my poetry." She lightly tapped her breastbone. "Inside, I am not so young-I have been through a lot, and my poetry reflects this. I have been divorced twice, Cali . . . I fear that I am not good in the long run." She laughed nervously. "You don't need a two-time loser, do you?"

"Don't you *dare* think of yourself, that way," I choked. "You're a three-time winner, and I love you."

Her face wavered, but her voice held steady. "I love you too, Cali, but we are from different lives, and I still have to work out parts of my past, through my poetry. You are focusing on what you feel right now, the idea of what you hope a future could bring us."

"But that *is* the essence of love!"

She sighed. "Perhaps . . . in fact, you are probably correct. Yet my own past experiences force me away from embracing such devotion. Do you recall what "The Bulgarian Poetess" noted of such hopes, such loves?"

I shook my head as I looked downward, eyes blurred.

"Actuality is a running impoverishment of possibility."

"Just one interpretation," I countered hollowly. "Time heals all wounds, Marti."

We sat and continued the debate for what was left of the afternoon. I lost. In the early evening, Marti and the legation boom-tubed to Purdue University.

In the ensuing weeks I functioned, but I really didn't live. I put out the minimum energy necessary to teach my classes, file for some grants, tutor a bit. Kashka Moravellov, of all people, became my sole source of emotional support. I made my departmental peace with him one November afternoon when I was seated in his office, receiving the third degree over a research proposal. He inadvertently quoted "The Checkist Of Alpha Prime" and I totally lost it, tearfully spilling the entire episode. Kashka produced a brandy bottle from his desk, did his utmost to console.

"Give her time, my dear young man," he softly advised, patting my wrist assuredly. "I know the Bulgarian heart-time can heal it the same as any other. If she feels the same as you do for her, she will overcome her painful past and reach out for you."

Two days before New Year's, Freddie visited me in my campus office.

"You got my kid's grade, yet?"

I looked up bleary-eyed amid stacks of finals. "Do I look like I'm anywhere *near* getting through this stuff?"

Freddie wrung his winter cap with both hands while giving me a puppy-dog look.

I sighed. "O.K., O.K. . . . go get a cup of coffee, it'll take me ten minutes to go through her stuff."

"Thanks, Cali-I'll sleep better, tonight. Oh, by the way-" he reached down to his feet, hefted up a cardboard container "-personal delivery from the shop-someone special ordered this for you. Didn't think you really knew anyone on Sofia."

Freddie left as I lifted the card out of the container. With trembling hands I unlatched the mahogany box, opened the halves partway.

I had absolutely no idea who the miniature woman was who spun and whirled about the desk; I'm sure that Freddie could have found out for me. But it didn't matter, really. All that counted was the meaning of the song that she belted out, a poetic quote written at least a century earlier, that held the most precious of personal messages for me:

> "... *Yes, I believe there comes a time,*
> *When everything must fall in line,*
> We live and learn from our mistakes,
> The deepest cuts are healed by fate . . .
> . . . Yes, I believe . . . "

I carefully closed the card and latched it, then put it back in its container. It took me about four seconds to slap a B-plus on Freddie's kid's final and seal it in an envelope. I picked up the card and a coat; after locking up, I taped the envelope to the outside of my office door. I hurried down the hallway in search of Kashka; a call to the Sofian consulate had to be made, a boom tube ticket had to be arranged. I had heard that immigrants were required to drop their surnames. I could live with that. There might be dozens of Cali's on Sofia, probably hundreds, just as there were hundreds of Marti's. Yet there was only one Marti in my life. And one Cali in hers.

Empty Houses

This is about the time that Mrs. Morita gave us back our freedom.

"Ma, I can't find the big wooden stirrin' spoon." I slammed the kitchen drawer in disgust. Or tried to, anyway; the damn thing squeaked to a halt, halfway to closing.

Ma was hunched over the kitchen table trying to hold Baby Suzette's chubby legs still for a brief moment. "Try the top drawer to the left of the sink," she replied distractedly around a mouthful of diaper pins.

"Neft 'o tink," Baby Suzette burbled.

"I already tried that drawer," I complained. "It ain't there."

"Well, that's where we kept it in the last house," Ma said softly, still unfocused.

"No *Ma,* we kept it in that drawer in the house *before* the last house!" Or was that the utensil drawer when we lived in last year's houses, I thought as I squatted and began to paw through the nearest cardboard moving box.

"Da nas *how!*" Baby Suzette shouted happily, as Ma finished diapering and hoisted her up to her shoulder.

Ma patted the baby's back as she stood surveying the cardboard wreckage of a still-arriving kitchen. She peered into the disheveled insides of a box that I was methodically gutting in search of my favorite Kool-Aid stirrer.

"I'm sorry our moves are a bit more messy these days, Pauli. Since Suzette's become more active, I just don't have the time to keep up our packing system the way I used to."

I sat back and looked up with a tinge of eleven-year-old guilt. "That's O.K., Ma-it ain't your fault. Popsy wanted me to code all of the kitchen stuff this move, but I just didn't get to any of it, what with the other stuff'n all."

Ma shook her head lightly, her rust-colored curls bobbing up and down as she moved about the kitchen, peering into various boxes. "Tell you what, my little man," she said as she reached down into a big one. "Next move, why don't you start packing and coding the kitchen stuff first-" she slightly puffed as she stood, adjusting Baby Suzette with her holding arm "-so that the royal Kool-Aid spoon is *never* far from hand!" She held the utensil out to me in triumph.

I grinned as I took it. "Thanks, Ma. I will." I stood up, began to stir the Kool-Aid pitcher on the counter. "I like this house, Ma. We haven't lived in a Colonial in awhile."

"That's right, Pauli. If your Popsy and I had our druthers, we'd live in a Colonial every time we move. Course, it's not always easy finding one with workable plumbing and wiring, and no broken windows to boot. We got real lucky finding this house."

I poured some Kool-Aid and gulped it down quick, then half-filled a plastic cup and held it out for Baby Suzette. She took it and slurped noisily. I turned and looked out the open window over the sink. "I'm gonna go throw a ball against the house next door."

"You stay off of that house's lawn," Ma shuddered. "Throw your ball from the street. You never know what kind of snakes are in there to bite, or rusty sprinklers to trip over."

A distant car horn wafted through the kitchen window on the morning breeze.

"Shave and a hair cut! Two bits!" Ma and I sang out together. "It's the Moritas!" I cried out happily.

I ran for the kitchen door, slamming it hard behind me.

"You be careful now, Pauli!" Ma called after me. "Stay in the streets, away from the lawns and sidewalks!"

"I will!"

"And give Mrs. Morita my best!"

"O.K., Ma!"

"The poor thing," I heard Ma say to herself more than to me.

I did as Ma said to and kept my running to the middle of the street. *Elm Street*, this one was called, and rightly so-the dead carcasses and dying remains of massive elms lined the way. It was easy running; the few downed tress had fallen back onto the buckled concrete sidewalks, their massive upper trunks mostly absorbed into the growing jungle entanglement of overgrown lawns. Even the street was in good shape, hardly any bumps or potholes. I knew Popsy would be happy that he'd be able to park our clunker right on the street where we lived.

I passed about a dozen empty houses with no sign of any life, then hit a bisecting street. *Spruce Lane*, the toppled sign proclaimed from the pavement. I spied a cul-de-sac about six houses downward. Mako was in one of the cul-de-sac driveways busily unpacking their clunker as Mister Morita stepped into an attached HUD-haul.

"Yo! Homeys!" I called out as I ran down the street and up the driveway.

Mako turned toward me, her young Japanese features lighting up in surprise and delight. "Yo! Home-*boy!*" she called back.

We happily punched each other in the upper arm-our non-throwing arms, of course. Mako and I were best friends back then, in an easy way that only a boy and a tomboy could be. We'd both been lucky for the opportunity to keep our friendship going-as fate would have it, we'd had the good fortune to end up in the same neighborhood during five of the last eight moves. However, it had been two moves since Mister Morita and Popsy had found usable houses near each other and I had really missed Mako-several months of separation seemed like an eternity when I was an eleven-year-old.

We had a lot of catching up to do and got right to it until Mrs. Morita called for Mako from inside the house.

Mako rolled her eyes. "She's more bizarre than usual, this move," she sighed. "I better go see what she's gotten herself into."

I nodded with understanding as Mako went inside-I knew it had to be tough watching over a crazy mother.

My attention was turned away as with a bump and a clunk, Mister Morita tripped out of the HUD-haul and plopped a heavy-looking box onto the driveway. He was a short, round man with a pencil-thin mustache and a glistening, Buddha-like face; as usual, he was heavily sweating inside a woolblend jacket and slacks, his heavy, Bavarian hunting hat perched forward on his head. ("Always wear shorts and a t-shirt when moving, Pauli," my Popsy would say. "God knows we do it enough, might as well be comfortable about it.") As always on Moving Day, Mister Morita looked uncomfortable. Sweaty uncomfortable. And somewhat bewildered.

He glanced at me with his version of recognition, then carefully knelt and began talking down into the box. "How are you, Pauli?"

"Fine, Mister Morita. Fine. And how are you?"

"Between befuddled and betwixted, Pauli," Mister Morita said to the box, then looked up at me with a serene smile. I couldn't help but smile back; Mister Morita was one of the nicest former homeless that I knew. Popsy, Ma and Mister Morita were the youngest of those who'd actually grown up homeless that I'd ever met. Most of the older ones had a certain wariness about'em, an edge of hardness and distrust that made me skittish to be near them. They seemed to need a lot of extra personal space. Course, given how rare it was to find usable houses next to each other, neighborly closeness wasn't often a problem.

"You folks settled in yet, Pauli?"

"Almost. My Popsy went back to San Bernardino for a final load."

"Every time," Mister Morita muttered, stacking already unloaded boxes at the side of the driveway. "I tell her to put the heavy stuff on the bottom of the boxes and the light stuff on top. But does she listen . . . "

He sat down on some boxes and wiped his brow with a handkerchief, going on with his oft-repeated moving complaints. I was thinking of saying something when Mister Morita suddenly fell silent as the porch door opened and Mrs. Morita trailed Mako outside.

She was a tall, beautiful slender woman with long, straight black hair and the smoothest skin I'd ever seen. She was also as daft as they come. Ma had told me once that Mrs. Morita's popsy had grown up rich. After her popsy was executed, the family became street people and Mrs. Morita went crazy; Mister Morita fell in love and married her, in spite of her problems. ("That's an important part of what love's all about, Pauli," Ma said then. "Feeling enough about a person so's to care for'em when they're down and out.")

Anyhow, the four of us stood there real quiet, Mako and Mister Morita all nervous and staring at me. *Say something nice and polite,* their eyes pleaded at me. *Make believe we can all be normal with her.*

"How are you doin' today, Mrs. Morita?" I ventured confidently.

The flame of insanity seemed to flicker higher than usual in Mrs. Morita's dark eyes as she gazed off into the distance. "I am far from the madding crowd today, Pauli. Far . . . from the madding crowd."

Mister Morita cleared his throat but for Mako's sake I beat him to it. "How do you like the new house, Mrs. Morita? Nice to find a Contemporary with workable plumbing for a change, ain't it?"

She continued to gaze off into the distance. "Our house . . . is a very, very *very* fine house . . . life used to be so hard."

"That's nice," I replied uncomfortably.

She seemed to snap out of it a bit, then; her face became a bit more normal. She looked at me. "Yes, Pauli. Very nice. Crosby, Stills . . . and someone else. Crosby . . . Stills . . . " She slipped back into the faraway look. "Patrick," she said to Mister Morita. "I'm going to take my morning walk, now."

"That's nice, dear," he replied with relief. "Just be careful."

Without another word, she meandered out of the driveway and down the street.

Mako and I stared at Mister Morita, who had knelt again and was pulling ceramic dishes out of a box. He held a big serving dish up for us to see. "Why in hell does she insist on making me lug all of this heavy stuff from house to house? I'm gonna slip a disk one of these days. Why can't we load light plastics like everyone else, huh?" He lowered his head as his shoulders began to shake. "Damn fool . . . has to have it her way or no way . . . "

Heavy tears began to drip down his face onto the cardboard box, making steady pattering sounds. Mako came up to him from behind and put her small arms around his quivering shoulders. "Don't worry, Popsy," she said confidently, slipping his hat off and laying her cheek on top of his head. "It's gonna be O.K.-this time, I found her spray paint and tossed it."

Whomp. "I got it."

Whomp. "Yours."

Whomp. "Mine."

Mako and I were whacking a ball off the back of the house next to hers. We had stomped down the waist-high grass behind the house to form a catching area; sides of houses were o.k., too, but this way my Ma wouldn't see us and have to worry.

Whomp. "Shit," I cursed.

Mako laughed as I missed the ball; I ran back and scooped it from behind before it disappeared into the overgrowth.

"Nice move, Home-Boy," Mako called out.

"Oh, yeah? You wanna see a nice move? Then watch this!" Aiming from way back deep at the edge of the catching area, I let loose with all I had. The rubber ball sailed up over the rain gutter, rolled smoothly up to the roof peak and quietly disappeared over to the front yard.

"Good goin', Pauli," Mako grinned.

"Shaddup, and help me go find it."

"Loser's weepers, Ace." Mako sat down cross-legged on the spot, closed her eyes and began to breathe steadily. I knew better than to ask for any help from her when she went into that meditation-thing.

I dropped my glove and headed for the driveway, keeping at least one eye downward, on the look-out for Ma's snakes and sprinklers. Turning the house corner, I looked up and stopped short.

Mrs. Morita had trampled a slender path up the lawn from the sidewalk to the house front. This particular Colonial had a large bay window leftward of the front door; she stood before the glass biting the tip of her tongue in concentration, steadily arcing a bright orange spray of lettering from the aerosol can in her right hand onto the glass.

As quietly as possible I trudged through the hip-high grass to the center of the yard. Mrs. Morita finished and stood back, both of us taking in her completed effort: *RODNEY KING* it read in neat lettering.

"There," she whispered. "That'll show'em-just *perfect.*"

She caught me in the window reflection, turned and smiled-she looked kind of o.k., for the moment.

"Hello, Pauli. I thought I heard you children in the back yard."

"Uh-huh. The ball came over the roof."

She smiled. "Did it now? I was too engrossed in my . . . art-work . . . I hadn't noticed." She pointed with a flourish. "What do you think?"

"It's uh, nice, Mrs. Morita, really . . . nice. What's it mean?"

"Mean?" She furrowed her brow in concentration, then bright-ened. "Why, it means . . . he's . . . a symbol of freedom, Pauli . . . he means . . . it means . . . "

She gently hung her head as tears filled her eyes. "It's not enough on its own, is it?"

"Um . . . I guess not." Agree with her, I thought-just keep her from freaking.

Suddenly her head snapped up, eyes focused upon me. "Do you know what day today is, Pauli?"

"Wednesday?"

"The calendar date?"

"Um-April 29?"

She smiled solemnly. "Correct-April 29. Do you remember what human tragedy began to unfold on April 29, thirty-one years ago?"

"Um-no."

She took on that far-off distant look again. "On April 29, 1992, the first of the rioting began over in Los Angeles." She peered up into the late afternoon sky; I followed her gaze up to a faint half-moon beginning to show among the blue. "I remember my grandmother's house in South Central . . . and the smoke, the fire . . . how the house burnt so . . . nothing left but gray steam and ash. But my mother's mother survived." She looked down the street. "As I shall survive all of this, Pauli. As shall we all. My grandmother wrote a haiku after the first wave of the riots ended." She closed her eyes and softly recited:

> "Now that my house has burned down,
> I have a much better view of the moon."

I stood still, waiting.

She opened her eyes and turned back to me.

"My artwork isn't enough, Pauli. We must do more for personal freedom. We must . . . we must *seize the day!* Yes . . . that's it! Seize the *day*, Pauli!"

Mrs. Morita closed her eyes, tilted her head back and let out a loud "Yip! Yip! Yahoo! *Yah!*" Then she tossed the aerosol can high in the air, and without another word trotted off the lawn and down the street.

I watched her round the corner and disappear from sight. "Fucked-up beyond belief," I muttered to myself as I began to search for the ball. A moment later Mako trotted around the house.

"Hey, that was neat, do it again!"

"What?"

"That Indian call-do it again."

"That wasn't me-it was your Ma." I pointed at the bay window.

Mako's eyes widened in worry as she took a step back. "I threw away her paint up in San Bernardino."

"Well, she got some more, somewhere." I pointed again at the window. "Who's Rodney King?"

"I don't know," Mako quavered. She put her face in her hands, began to talk around sobs. "She's getting crazier . . . our last house was near one of those Homeowner's Association subdivisions, they kept watch on us a lot . . . they got real mad when she sprayed that 'Rodney King' name on a window next door . . . said they'd take her away to a hospital if she didn't stop it . . . "

I put my arm around Mako's trembling shoulder, spoke through my own fear. "It's gonna be all right, Mako-I promise. You have us and you have your popsy. No one's gonna take away your Ma."

She nodded in fearful agreement, then turned and buried her wet face in my shoulder. "I promise, Mako," I whispered. "No one'll take her away."

We stood there like that for awhile until Mako stopped crying, then pulled away as we heard the distant staccato honking of a clunker announcing a new homey family arrival in the neighborhood. Mako wiped her cheeks with her palms and snuffled as we abandoned the yard, ball and paint can in search of our newest neighbors.

Popsy got in from San Bernardino with the last load around dusk that night. Ma had invited the Moritas to supper and we were all seated around the table in our new kitchen.

"You cut it close, Jason," said Mister Morita. "I wouldn't want to be circling around the Moreno Valley looking for my new house after dark."

Popsy nodded in agreement. "I needed to get a few things out of the old place, today. That broken pipe had saturated through the first floor ceiling, was flooding the living room."

Just then Baby Suzette squealed from her high chair and tossed handfuls of food about the room. Mako and I laughed as Ma picked her up and began to clean about. "Honestly, I don't know what's been getting into this child today! All day, it's throw this and throw that! It seems like what little toilet training we've managed went out the door-"

"It's the move," I said around a mouthful of mashed potatoes.

The adults around the table stopped eating just then, eyeing me uncomfortably.

"What do you mean?" asked Mako as we both continued eating.

"Suzette's always cranky when we move. She gets settled and used to the last place and hates to leave."

"Sounds like you had no choice in the matter," replied Mako. "What with the waterpipe bursting."

"It started as just a little leak," I replied distractedly around a drumstick. "Popsy had more than a week to find this house and start us to packing before it really let loose.

"By the way," I asked Mako. "What busted in your last place?"

"A fuse."

I stopped chewing and looked at her, puzzled. "A what?"

"A fuse. It's a little round glass thing in that metal box on the outside of the house."

"That's enough now, Mako," said Mister Morita gently.

Mako ignored him and began to speak more rapidly building up speed as if she was afraid of being interrupted. "The thing is, I really loved that house-the water pressure was great, with lots of hot water. And the windows and electrical generator were also really good. I bet they could've lasted years! Then we were reading one night last week and all the lights went out. Popsy had one of those Homeowner's Association people come over and check the next morning and he said one of the fuses had burnt out-"

"Mako," warned Mister Morita.

She ignored him, frantically picking up the tempo. "-and we started packing. And the thing of it is, I loved that house so much, there was this busted-up old library down the street and I found some old books still in there and I took'em home but Popsy said we didn't have enough room in the HUD-haul so I had to leave'em in the old house-"

"Mako!" Mister Morita repeated with uncharacteristic sternness.

Mako's eyes filled as she looked at me pleadingly and plowed on. "-and I just keep thinking it was only a dumb little fuse, there were dozens of'em like brand new in these little boxes in the garage and why couldn't we just take out the broken one and put in a new one but Popsy said-"

Just then Mister Morita said something curtly to Mako in Japanese.

"Screw you, you jerk!" Mako cried-out at Mister Morita, banging her fist on the table. Dishes rattled as we all stared. "I loved our home and that library and those books! It was just a tiny fuse, a stupid little thing!" She pointed at my Popsy. "He could've fixed the waterpipe when it was just a little leaky! You could've replaced the damn fuse! Why do we all have to move all the time!"

I sat staring at the adults as Mako ran crying onto the back porch, slamming the kitchen door hard behind her. Baby Suzette gazed about in wide-eyed baby anticipation as the adults unfroze and calmly turned back to eating dinner.

"Once a house is broke, it's broke," said Popsy pleasantly as he steadily ate. "No two ways about it."

"That's the old homey saying, all right," replied Mister Morita, nodding and swallowing.

On the back porch I found Mako wiping her tears, looking back in through the porch window. "Look at'em," she glared, chin set in defiance. "They don't care." She turned and headed off the porch. "I'm going home-I mean, back to the new house."

While Ma washed the supper dishes I told her and Popsy about Mrs. Morita's graffitti.

"Mrs. Morita's been through an awful lot over the years," said Popsy.

"It's these empty houses," Ma grimaced, rattling table plastics in frustration.

"Now, Evelyn-" Popsy tried to sooth.

"Don't 'now Evelyn' me," Ma snapped. "It's a wonder more of us aren't like Ikuyo!" She took a deep breathe and shook her head. "Maybe Mako's right, Jason," she said quietly. "We act like we're still living on the streets, moving around to stay alive. Maybe this time we could stay in one place a little longer, replace the fuse or fix the little leak, take a little responsibility."

"Responsibility," Popsy replied flatly. "First it's a fuse change or a leak plugged. Then we start putting more roots down as fixing the place up and changing things, adding to'em begins to take over." He moved closer to Ma. "You want your kids living in one place forever, packed like sardines into side-by-side houses? You want to end up living behind the iron gates of some . . . some Homeowner's Association subdivision? You want to give up our freedom-our way of life?

Ma's face turned an angry crimson. "Freedom . . . way of life? You call moving around the old towns a way of life? We don't make homes here-we need a real, living community to be a part of, Jason, with neighbors and churches and ballfields, not empty houses for our kids to throw balls against! If not for us, at least for Pauli and Suzette! Living among empty houses breeds empty souls!"

I didn't dare breathe as Ma and Popsy glared at each other.

Then Ma spoke in almost a whisper. "Who's going to go crazy next, Jason?"

I was the one who broke the seemingly endless silence. "What's that smell, Ma?"

The three of us looked at each other; a puff of evening breeze through the kitchen door seemed to kick it up. We heard the clunker horn just as the realization of it hit home for all of us; three short honks followed by three long ones, repeated over and over-the distress signal of the moving families.

"Fire," Ma whispered fearfully, scooping Baby Suzette up off of the kitchen floor. I didn't even hear Popsy's reply, only the kitchen door slam as I bolted out, alone with the fearful thought burning over and over in my brain: *Mako.*

The ash was funneling down Spruce Street as I reached the cul-de-sac. Mister Morita sat in the open clunker door. frantically pounding away on the car horn with one hand and mopping his brow with a handkerchief. Mako stood open-mouthed and mesmerized in the driveway, watching the house next door.

Unless I was really off-base, Mrs. Morita must have gotten her hands on some gasoline-maybe she siphoned off the clunker tank. The upper floor of the house next to the Morita's was aburst with orange flame, waves of black smoke rippling higher still. Mrs. Morita stood on the front lawn, waiting expectedly as I drew near. She pointed at the rapidly heating bay window. The *Rodney King* graffitti collapsed inward as the flames licked down.

"Why, Mrs. Morita?" I tugged her sleeve to get her farther away from the heat. She took a few steps back, then stopped and looked at me with fresh sanity.

"I did this for my Mako, Pauli. And for you and Suzette."

The fires of freedom flickered higher in her now-sane eyes, as she gazed at the billowing roof.

I suddenly thought of her grandmother's haiku, and whispered it to myself:

"Now that my house has burned down,
I have a much better view of the moon."

I managed to pull her back to the street as Popsy and the new neighbors pulled up and rushed by us to help Mister Morita and Mako evacuate as much of their stuff as possible.

"What do we do now, Mrs. Morita?"

She turned toward me and placed a firm hand on my shoulder.

"Now, Pauli, we build our own house. Our own home."

Sparks were clustering higher on the night breeze. By the end of the week, most of the Moreno Valley subdivisions had burned to the ground.

Okura turned four years old last summer. On a humid, early August night at dusk, I took her small hand in mine and we walked for several blocks along clean, smooth concrete sidewalks illuminated by soft street lights, past neatly-manicured lawns ahush with the shushing of summer sprinklers. Here and there we passed the

partially completed husks of new homes arising. We passed a
ballfield where children called out to Okura and she called back
laughingly to them.

After awhile, we came to the burnt remains of the house. Okura
clutched my hand tighter.

"Kinda spooky, Popsy."

"Every neighborhood has one, honey."

"Why, Popsy?"

"It's a symbol to remind us, honey-of where we all came up
from, and how you have to stand up for personal freedom."

"What's personal freedom, Popsy?"

I hoisted Okura up onto my shoulders and began to stroll
homeward. "Let's go home and have some Kool-Aid in those new
ceramic mugs that your grandfather made; then I will tell you all
about your Grandmother Ikuyo and the empty houses . . . and
personal freedom . . . and the view of the moon."

We Got The Funk!

"Now let me get this straight," says Geraldine to Doctor Harry, her high heels clicking a steady backbeat as they walk together down the inner city street, martini glasses balanced in hand. "You say we're not in Philadelphia, anymore? We're in some town called Rockwell?"

Doctor Harry halts and shakes his head of thinning gray hair, samples his martini while gazing into Geraldine's lovely, young bright blue gams.

"Not exactly, my dear. As I told you earlier at the department social hour, we're in what I've come to refer to during my previous visits here as a 'Norman Rockwell reality.'" They continue to walk and sip. "As the new physics department secretary, you've quickly shown a remarkable proclivity, my dear, for both discretion and respect regarding the various faculty members' shall we say "eccentric" research projects. As such, I felt that you would appreciate my own personal research project and that I would in turn receive from you a certain level of, shall we say, discrete confidence regarding my own pet project."

Doctor Harry pauses and drains the last of his martini. "Have I ever told you how much you look like my ex-wife Edna when she and I first married?"

"Three times at the party, Doc," Geraldine says distractedly as she looks around the neighborhood of red brick buildings. She drains the last of her own martini and tosses back her luxurious red hair out of her lovely blue gams. "Say Doc, what is it that's different about this street? I can't quite put my finger on it."

The neighborhood around them is pulsing with normal afternoon city street activity, of kids playing stickball between the traffic, people running errands and neighbors chatting on apartment building stoops.

"It's quite simple, my dear," says Doctor Harry as they resume walking, this time hand-in-hand. "While the good Doctor Hostedler and his team have focused their research efforts on time travel, I've focused my team's efforts toward parallel travel. In extremely simple laymen's terms, rather than gaining the ability to move backwards or forwards in the timestream, my parallel chamber has allowed us to move sideways outside of our own timestream into a parallel existing timestream, as such providing us with the ability to experience alternate yet almost similar worldframes, so to speak."

Geraldine smiles playfully at Doctor Harry and fingers the left shoulder strap of her cocktail dress. "Seems your invitation to slip away from the party and see your private chamber wasn't exactly what I expected, Doc."

Doctor Harry blushes furiously. "Er, I, um, believe I said parallel chamber, not private, my dear. When you said that you admired the Norman Rockwell print hanging in the faculty lounge, I said that we could visit the original via my parallel chamber."

Geraldine's face brightens through the martini-induced haze. "Hey, that's right! You said you had the original of the Rockwell in your room!" She looks around again, puzzled. "So why are we out here, and again, what's bugging me about this neighborhood?"

Doctor Harry's blush subsides as with a professorial flourish he proceeds to expound as they continue walking, this time arm-in-arm. "Correction, my dear. As I tried to briefly explain through the chit-chat din of the social, via the act of entering and activating my parallel chamber, we have emerged into a side reality similar yet in ways different from our own. In a word, we are in a *version* of Philadelphia, walking a *version* of the nearby city streets just outside a *version* of our own dear university's inner city urban campus.

"What is 'buggin' you, as you say, about the neighborhood are its variations that, you may notice, make it somewhat different in this reality stream from our own. Whereas this neighborhood street in our own 1995 timestream holds a distinct flavor of late-20th century American inner city decay and decline, the neighborhood that we currently stroll in this 1995 alternate timestream strangely enough holds what our world considers a mid-20th century American culture and population demographic." Doctor Harry waves his hand airily about his head. "Hence the abnormalities that you would be able to more readily put your finger on, so to speak, if we both weren't so pickled with martini, my dear. The period clothes. The cars. The whitebread population. Circa 1945 in our world, I would say."

Geraldine has been gazing at Doctor Harry during all of this with her mouth hanging open and her eyes glazed in a fair imitation of a mackeral on ice. She snaps out of it when he comes up for air.

"No shit," she replies.

Doctor Harry sighs as they resume walking, this time with their arms around each other's waist. "Well, actually . . . some shit."

"Come again?"

"There seems to be two extremely odd abnormal social activity clusters occurring in this neighborhood. We've documented several instances of both types over the course of numerous visits."

"What might that be, Doc?"

"The first is quite pleasant to observe, actually," says Doctor Harry as his fingers climb to absently fiddle with the back of Geraldine's left shoulder strap.

"It seems that periodically, if one is in the right place and of keen eye, one can observe an extraordinary activity of the neighborhood residents playing-out a moment of their daily routine exactly as depicted in one of the paintings completed by the artist Norman Rockwell, whom we both greatly admire in our own timestream. The second seems to be an odd mix of what you and I would consider 1970's American culture popping up in this distinctly mid-twentieth century mileau. Before we leave today, I'd like to further investigate the second-"

Doctor Harry stops fingering Geraldine's shoulder strap as she halts and laughs. "Come on, Doc. This is a joke, right? You can't believe that you walk around here while different Saturday Evening Post covers pop-up in real life?"

"Oh yes, it's quite true," says Doctor Harry. "I and various team members have observed the phenomenon quite a few times.

We've even gotten ahead of the game by researching through Rockwell's paintings in our own world and scouting-out potential background locations in this neighborhood, then waiting in observation until the scene briefly plays-out in the residents' behavior."

Geraldine laughs again and shakes her head. "Look, you don't have to bullshit me this way to try to impress me, Doc. You're O.K. in my book in your own way—"

"No, the phenomenon is true, please believe me." Doctor Harry gently takes Geraldine's wrist and leads her toward a nearby building corner. "As I said, we've gotten a step ahead of the game. Just look down that alley and I'm sure you'll see what I mean."

Geraldine peers around the building corner and stops breathing for a moment, then takes a deep breath and takes a step forward.

The alley is fairly wide with a few scraps of wood and bits of paper strewn about in the otherwise clean dirt. Along the left side of the alley, two wooden tenement stoops serve a faded cluster of red brick apartments, green paint peeling off of the old porch wood. Two tall, mostly dead trees stand two stories high as sentries aside one of the old wooden stoops. Two young boys sit in the dying branches of one tree, chatting with a boy perched in the other tree. The alley is otherwise mostly empty, save for a red-haired man wearing faded khaki workclothes and matching cap perched on the roof of the first stoop, steadily hammering in new planks; a pretty, blonde teenaged girl wearing a plain green dress with white sleeves and a red bow in her hair stands below, idly watching the man on the roof.

"This can't be real," whispers Geraldine.

"Ah, but it is very real, my dear," says Doctor Harry as he comes up behind Geraldine and places his hands on her shoulders. "The backdrop for 'Homecoming Soldier.' Saturday Evening Post Editor Ben Hibbs considered it the greatest magazine cover ever published. He hung the original over his desk. You've enjoyed viewing the copy hanging in our faculty lounge. And now you and

I have the distinct pleasure of witnessing the wonderful painting come to life."

Doctor Harry consults his watch. "My team has held discreet conversation with some alley residents this past week. We should be right about on time, if our review of the local train schedule was correct." He peers back around the alley corner into the street. "Ah, here he comes, now."

Geraldine turns just as a young, red-haired serviceman enters the alley, no more than a boy, actually, fresh-faced and excitedly nervous in his tight dress uniform, small duffel bag clenched tightly in his left hand.

"'Scuse me, Ma'am," the boy squeaks, barely glancing at Geraldine as he quickly strides past her up the alley, a huge, excited grin on his face. Geraldine and Doctor Harry turn to watch the boy, just as the kids in the trees spot him and start shouting.

And then in the next moment it happens, just as Rockwell painted it.

The man working atop the roof turning in delight. The porch stoop exploding with three happily shrieking red-haired moppets and a panting beagle, all racing down the steps toward the homecoming soldier boy. The thrilled parents coming out onto the porch, mother's arms wide open in homecoming welcome. The happy neighbors crowding the stoop and windows of the adjacent red brick building. The blonde high school sweetheart, back straight against the building corner wall, shyly peering at the returned boyfriend.

Tears well in both Geraldine's and Doctor Harry's eyes as the scene holds for a brief moment, then motions onward as the family and neighbors cluster around the boy in hugs, pats and kisses.

"Cool," says Geraldine as she dabs her eyes with a lipstick-stained tissue.

"Yes, quite cool," replies Doctor Harry as he blows his nose into a monogrammed handkerchief.

Geraldine turns to Doctor Harry and smiles sweetly, then moves forward and quickly kisses him on the lips. "Thanks, Doc. That was quite a kick." She takes his arm as they slowly stroll toward the alley entrance. "What say we head home through that chamber of yours, Doc? I've got a coffeetable book of Rockwell's stuff over at my place that I'd like to show you."

"A wonderful idea, my dear," replies Doctor Harry, once again blushing furiously. "I believe my team can further investigate by itself that second cultural abnormality that I mentioned earlier-"

Doctor Harry's words are cut off as a sonic crash of live music erupts from back in the alley. He and Geraldine whirl around in time to see the dancing band emerge into the other end of the alley, heading toward the homecoming scene. A mix of high strutting black and white performers, male and female alike, wildly dancing bandmembers peppered with a blaring horn section, all wearing bright horns and huge hats, shaking tambourines and holding aloft a large paper-mache and tinfoil mock flying saucer, the entire jiving action led in-time by a dancing, hopping, grinning black man in dark shades and rainbow dreadlocks.

"It can't be," repeats a stunned Geraldine.

"I actually think it is," replies Doctor Harry.

"George Clinton And The Parliament Funkadelic," they say in unison. Then look at each other in mutual surprise.

Dance to the music, all night long . . . the band reaches the homecoming crowd and the two groups intermingle with natural ease . . . *everyday people sing a simple song . . .* band members, family and neighbors together hoist the soldier boy atop shared shoulders as the tempo increases . . . *I want to thank you for everything you've done . . .*

"You know," says Doctor Harry. "I cut quite a funkadelic rug at faculty socials back in the seventies."

"I know my older sister's entire Sly And The Family Stone collection by heart," replies Geraldine. They stare at each other a moment, then both slyly grin. "Come on, Doc, let's show'em what we got. We'll get to my coffeetable book, yet."

Holding hands, Geraldine and Doctor Harry fling their empty martini glasses skyward and run down the alley toward the celebration, as with a *Boom Shacka Lacka Lacka!* a conga line starts to form.

Flagship Of The Gods

I write as reflex, knowing in my heart that Michael's nearby efforts underway at this moment will most likely transform this paper into useless ash by dawn.

So many words. So little time. Yet I must try, the not-so-distant night sounds of Cairo urging me onward. Evening spotlights bathe the nearby face of the Sphinx in gaudy tourist pastels. There is little comfort in reasoning that the scowl on the ancient's face is an illusion resulting from the poor angle of lighting.

Far easier to embrace the illusion, lean upon it as the final crutch with which to face denouement. Michael's denouement. Our denouement.

You modern fool, Susan, the ancient Pharoah-god whispers on the night breeze. *You could have stopped this. This abomination.*

I could not try. My love for Michael blinded me, led me to fervently believe that his quest was harmless, would merely result in satisfaction derived from the journey traveled, not the end result.

I believe that our love will surely save us. I truly do. I do. I hope. Oh, dear God, help us.

Fool, the Sphinx softly sighs yet again in the night. *Your blind love has damned us all.*

I write faster, the scratching of the pen barely covering the ancient's recriminations.

I could have diverted Michael away from stepping onto his path at the beginning, back when we first fell in love, when we were both graduate research assistants. But I was too in love to hurt him and while his theory was considered crackpot I supported him emotionally even in this, the holy grail quest, the Chariots Of The Gods picture puzzle illusion. I beamed and nodded in support as he confided in me that first time the details of his recently-begun quest to follow the ancient riddle for its answer.

"I found the first piece of the puzzle in a fragment of hieroglyphic off a broken sarcophagus recovered last year from the pyramid of Chephren," he confided one night. "It was so obvious, the reference to instructions from the ancient visitors. So clear. If only one *believes,*" he whispered fiercely. "Believes like me."

And believe Michael did. In the ultimate message from ancient visitors to the ancient Egyptians. And on to us. Through Michael.

He continued to follow the path year by year, partial clue by fragmented hint, all scattered about the Giza Plateau like an ancient giant child's abandoned playthings. Seven years ago the Chephren clue led Michael to the King's Chamber in the nearby pyramid of Mycerinus. His reinterpretation of certain hieroglyphics led to Mycerinus's grandfather's tomb, the imposing pyramid of Cheops himself. Through the ancient king's burial chamber high within the pyramid, the path wound deep into the ascending ancient structural repair chambers, up through the Dawson chamber, Wellington, higher yet into Nelson, upward to Arbuthnot into Campbell, the forehead chamber. There among the graffiti scribblings of ancient workmen, Michael found the clearest path sign yet. Pointed steeply downward. Into the shattered workmen's settlements covered deep beneath the Giza Plateau below.

For three expeditions, Michael followed the path through the winding worker's settlement quarters. Last year, the final road sign.

A section of hieroglyphic fragment found in the settlements revealed itself to be part of the missing text from the Pillar of Tutmos IV, Tutankhamen's great-grandfather and first restorer of the Sphinx, the feline god already 1200 years old in his day.

"It's the Sphinx, by God!" he laughed upon his return to our home. "I always felt it was connected, even though the old sonars were negative! It's probably shielded in some extraterrestrial material that belied the readings!"

This time I was part of the expedition that arrived here 70 days ago, in expectation of being with Michael as his long trail finally, fruitlessly petered-out.

Michael and his team wasted no time examining the three known passageways into the Sphinx. Dig deep and long, his precious clue advised, and that they did. Two weeks ago, they struck the buried passageway leading not into the ancient icon but beneath it; the cat god lay as sentry above the chamber secreted deep in the world below.

The expedition has spent the past several days analyzing the chamber below, the unidentifiable metals and equipment, the almost overwhelming mix of alienness hidden beneath this ancient human setting. Yet it is the true final clue that has kept me on the surface this evening to scrawl in the sand by the Sphinx paws, the hieroglyphic that framed the ancient seal which blocked that final chamber, a message utterly ignored by all save me as Michael and the team rushed to break through into the chamber beyond.

I know Michael too well, saw the lie in his eyes as he laughed reassuredly to me a mere hour ago, before the final descent to attempt activation. "Visitors I believe in, curses are for fools," he reassured. "An ancient king's metaphor, nothing else."

And yet his look belied his laugh, his choice of words supporting my dread. Why define the ancient words as curse, why dismiss the hieroglyphic as useless metaphor when metaphor guided Michael successfully along the path?

He has journeyed too far alone, my love, intoxicated beyond reason by the discovered excitements at this end.

Casting useless pen and paper aside, I grasp fistfuls of desert sand, toss them futilely toward the mocking Sphinx, heave more fistfuls at the desert sky. I halt, entranced by the blazing starbeds awash in the deep desert night sky.

Another curse comes to mind, a story of discovery, the final perceptions of God in another place, another time. The stars sit motionless, waiting. Over long minutes my dread retreats, transforms into its final form of inevitability.

I speak my version of the final name of God, the warning from below: "He Who Partakes Of The Bounty Within Shall Move The World Onto The Path Toward Heaven."

The Sphinx screams into the night as Michael succeeds. The stars remain in the sky this time, as the world takes a shaking first step onto the ancient path, beginning a journey trailblazed by Michael, toward the heaven of the gods.

"Literally," I whisper as the stars sit in place, waving us goodbye.

Thin Ice

I call her Torvill.

She calls me Dean.

Peanut calls me the Pumpkin King, says I will bring "an exquisite sense of celebratory wonder" to both his species and mine "at the appropriate time." Peanut ignores my questions regarding Svetlana.

"She serves her purpose," he mumbles when I press the issue. Or at least I interpret the response echoing from the voice orifice centered in the lower half of his peanut-shaped body as a mumble.

"We take her not for her, but for you . . . to elevate you to be exquisite at the appropriate time." Peanut's voice orifice emits a series of sighs and whispers, his reed-thin arm appendages gesturing across the rink toward where Svetlana awaits, as distanced from Peanut as she can get within the ship rink's confine.

"Now go, Jimmy. To her. Skate."

I have no choice in the matter. Glancing up through ship's dome at Earth suspended above, I cross the ice to her. Peanut sits alone in the rink's peanut gallery, his solitary expectations unfathomable as always.

We skate.

Svetlana. My Torvill.

Like a high-strung colt she is energetically working her way through a solo routine as I cross the ice. Triple lutz/double toe combination. Triple salchow. Triple toe loop. She stumbles badly on the toe loop. The snatch has taken more of a toll on her psyche than on mine.

It was more in my nature to expect a situation such as this from arriving aliens. First Contact did include the obligatory B-movie scenes, of delegations of Peanuts at the White House, a Peanut presentation at the United Nations, commentaries from reverential television commentators describing advanced alien technologies and sciences.

For me, it was the aliens' fascination with certain human physical activities that was most unexpected, and which was met with a fair amount of alien bemusement. Confined in their dumpy Mister Peanut bodies, the aliens seemed obsessed with any human activities that required a highly refined degree of athletic body precision and grace. Ballet. Competitive high dive. Gymnastics. And there was figure skating.

They flipped-out over figure skating, attending all of the pro events and road shows, trading technology information for miles of performance tapes from the networks. When pressed by the media for reasoning of their obsession, the explanation was always the same: potential that they might one day experience "exquisiteness" through figure skating. No further explanation was given.

The call came from the U.N. late one October evening, just after I got off the Ice Capades ice at Madison Square Garden. A Peanut wanted to meet me. I went down to their landing facilities by the World Trade Center, met with the one that Svetlana and I would come to simply consider as Peanut.

Peanut was very complimentary. "We see you as having the highest potential for assisting us in experiencing exquisiteness." I replied that I was flattered, but that I personally disagreed; I had never taken an Olympic or championship medal, and was just winding-down my career in the Ice Capades.

"Pairs will bring out your potential on ice."

I laughed. "Pairs? I've never skated pairs competitively, only in a few exhibition shows."

Peanut swiveled and lumbered toward the room wall. "Pairs will elevate you, bring us exquisiteness." He emitted a series of sighs and whistles into a wall communicator. The door opened and another Peanut came through with Svetlana. Both Peanuts focused their upper eyes series on me expectedly as I gazed at Svetlana. I had only seen her once before from a distance, at a road show last year outside of Odessa. On the ice she was graceful and heartbreaking. Off the ice she was stunningly beautiful.

"You like?" Peanut asked me.

"I . . . admire," I replied as Svetlana and I smiled to each other, extending hands.

"Good," said Peanut. "We will all go, now."

Svetlana and I both blacked-out then, awakening at some later time on-ship in earth orbit.

Svetlana halts her routine as I near, afixes me with hopeful blue eyes. "Well, Jimmy?" she asks in accent-tinged English. "Did it shed any light on the situation?"

I shake my head no. "It still emphasizes me. Says you will assist me in allowing them to experience exquisiteness through me."

She lowers her chin as I speak, then snaps her head up to glare defiantly at me, eyes half-filled with tears. Cursing rapidly in Russian, she turns and races across the rink toward Peanut. I follow, catching Svetlana just as she reaches the peanut gallery. I grab her waist from behind as she is about to leap off-ice at an impassive Peanut. Svetlana stops struggling and shouting as Peanut raises himself up, upper eye series affixing over her shoulder at me.

"You do not share her language?"

"She shares mine."

"A pity. So colorful. And unique, this concept of multiple languages within one race. So rare, to experience first-hand."

"I don't need a translator to know what she wants. What we both want. We want out. Bring us home."

Peanut's lower eye series begin to blink rapidly. "When you achieve exquisiteness, we will give to you the one desire that you ask of us."

"Just what the fuck do you mean by 'exquisiteness'!"

Peanut ignores Svetlana and keeps staring at me, lower eyes continuing to blink rapidly. "When you achieve exquisiteness, we will give to you the one desire that you ask of us."

"Give us some direction, here," I plead. "Do you expect perfect triples? A quadruple axel? What!"

"When you achieve exquisiteness, we will give to you the one desire that you ask of us."

It's no use. Peanut's in broken record mode, repeats himself in answer to any of our further curses or pleadings. His voice echoes in accompaniment to Svetlana's rising curses as I drag her across and off the ice to our quarters.

Svetlana sighs, props herself up on her left elbow while self-consciously covering her breasts with the bedsheet. "So the thing is referring to you, Jimmy."

Still lying on my back I reach around her slender neck, cup her ponytail in my hand. "That much is obvious."

She shakes me off while reaching over my head to the wall alcove for a cigarette, quickly lights-up. Nicotine in hand, Svetlana drops her self-consciousness and the sheet, sits up in bed cross-legged toward me.

"It utterly ignores me, Jimmy. You are the one it wants to achieve this 'exquisiteness' for them. And when you achieve it, you will be given the one desire that you ask of it." She exhales twin smoke streams through her nostrils, gazes at me worriedly.

I stroke her thigh. "So what? My one desire is for us to go home" Svetlana continues to silently stare at me worriedly. "Both of us. That's the magic wish."

She flicks ash on the bed, shakes her head rapidly. "You may not necessarily ask for us to go home."

I laugh. "You've got to be kidding! Why in God's name would I ask for anything else! The fuckers kidnapped us! All the alien magic gifts there are couldn't get me to stay with these things!"

Svetlana climbs out of bed and softly pads across the room, halts with arms folded across her breasts to stare forlornly into the wall mirror. I follow and wrap my arms around her from behind, stare ahead at our paired mirror image. "Don't worry, my sweet Torvill," I whisper. "I have a gut feeling. They have their own alien sense of 'borrowing' us for awhile. They'll put us back after we put on a great performance for them to add to their tape collection."

Svetlana sighs heavily and reaches down to squeeze my arm around her waist. "I too have a gut feeling, Jimmy Dean. I do not believe they want us . . . you . . . to go. They will grant your wish, but make it so that you ask differently."

"Impossible."

She turns and stares deep into my eyes. "They did not take you just for your skating, Jimmy, you know you are just average professional, now. There's some other quality in you that intrigues them. I will bet you a ruby that we aren't going anywhere."

Peanut always chooses our practice music, plays it for us once on the rink's audio system and then instructs us to use it in the practice session. Yesterday we had skated wonderfully to a medley from the rock opera "Tommy." Today we practiced poorly to "It's Time To Face The Music And Dance!" Svetlana stalked off the ice in mid-routine cursing in her native language, leaving Peanut and I together at rinkside.

"You should let us stick with 'Tommy,' Peanut. We'll be able to put on a great performance with it."

Peanut whistles and sighs. "Why does the music matter?"

"The music is crucial, Peanut. We perform to it. It sets the tone, creates a link to the audience for them and us to experience the performance together."

Peanut is momentarily silent as he digests this, then in an all-too-recognizable human motion shakes his upper body half side-to-side. "We disagree. As your audience, we will link with you differently."

I'm intrigued with this alien perception, and press for insight. "We play the music only for you, Jimmy. We link with you through the heart. Your performance emotion will allow us to experience exquisiteness."

"Then we're ready," I reply. "We'll perform tomorrow. To 'Tommy.'" I hesitate, then plunge ahead. "And then I'll ask my one wish. And you'll grant it."

Peanut's lower eye series renew their disconcerting blinking habit. "No need to be concerned, Jimmy Dean. Your wish will be granted."

"I'll tell Svetlana, then. We perform tomorrow."

"One question before you go, Jimmy."

I wait expectedly.

"Are you familiar with your English language expression 'being on thin ice'?"

I nod uneasily.

"Good. Good. It will aid your performance, tomorrow. Help us to experience exquisiteness. Good day, Jimmy."

I skate across the rink, an anxious feeling beginning to knaw in my gut. At rink's edge I pause and turn back. Peanut remains standing, watching me. His mouth orifice silently smiles. In an all-too-recognizable human way, the smile doesn't appear to be friendly.

Sleep is extremely difficult for us this night. Svetlana and I lay in bed steadily talking through the evening about the situation, the future, the performance. At last, we nervously drift off.

In the ship's morning, I awake alone. In rising panic, I quickly dress and traverse nearby corridors toward the rink in search of Svetlana. Partway there, I turn a corridor and come face-to-face with Peanut.

"Where is she, Peanut."

He turns and begins lumbering down a side corridor. "She is being prepared for your performance. Come. You need to be prepared."

I follow as we enter a small dressing room. I notice as I comply with Peanut's request to change into skating garb and don skates that a small video unit perches on the dresser counter. As I finish dressing, Peanut waddles over by the unit and swivels to face me.

"She told you that we did not take you for your skating alone, Jimmy."

"You bugged our bedroom."

Peanut ignores me and continues. "She is correct. You are an average skater, Jimmy." An arm appendage snakes out to caress the unit. "We traded for many tapes, reviewed thousands of hours seeking potential for exquisiteness. At last, we found a tape that identified that potential. In you." Peanut's arm appendage moves and activates the unit. The screen flickers alive.

The tape is from last year's exposition. In Odessa. A network camera kept rolling as the performance ended, recording the scene as local skaters intermingled on the ice with the show performers. I recognize myself on the ice, from time-to-time see glimpses of Svetlana at a distance from me. The tape ends.

I look at Peanut, baffled. "I don't get it. We're not even performing."

"Watch again." Peanut's arm appendage hovers by the unit, hitting control pads. The tape begins to play anew. Peanut freezes the tape. On me, as I am skating off the ice. "What do you see, Jimmy?"

"Nothing in particular. Just me skating off the ice."

Peanut whistles and sighs. "Watch carefully." Peanut manipulates the scene forward frame-by-frame . . . I skate slowly from center ice toward the edge of the Odessa rink . . . I turn my head to the right . . . the camera pans to my right . . . the camera takes in a figure, Svetlana as she heads off the ice . . . the camera pans back across the ice, settles in on me for a moment then pans off to the emptying arena seats. Peanut rewinds the tape a few frames to stop on me. "There."

"There what? It's just me! Looking across the ice as I leave!"

Peanut's lower eyes renew their blinking habit. "Yes. There. Across the ice."

I stare at the screen, at my face as comprehension dawns. On screen I am staring across the ice. At Svetlana. In normal playtime it happens quickly and doesn't register well. In freeze frame the look on my face is obvious. Very obvious.

Blushing furiously, I turn to peanut. "You kidnapped us because I was attracted to Svetlana?!"

Peanut trundles toward the dressing room exit. "Your human emotion for her was true and obvious. Your reaction to the situation will be evident in your performance." Peanut rolls into the corridor. "Go now, Pumpkin King. Your Sally awaits you. Skate. Be exquisite."

An icy chill racks me as I leave the room and head toward the rink. I clambor up the entrance ramp toward rinkside amidst a rising chorus of whistles and sighs; the peanut gallery is filled to capacity with expectant Peanuts. Distracted by the crowd seated about me, I don't look ringside until I've removed my blade guards and hopped onto the ice. Then I look about me and see Svetlana. I vaguely remember beginning to scream before passing out.

Peanut has pumped me full of something that revives me and helps me to function, with the exception of one small piece of me that keeps on steadily screaming, deep down inside. I steady myself at the edge of the ice, staring at Peanut to avoid looking at the crowd or Svetlana.

"Why?" I hear myself ask hoarsely.

Both sets of Peanut's eyes begin blinking rapidly. "Because you are our Pumpkin King." He waves an arm appendage beyond my shoulder. "Your emotion for here . . . for this . . . will be expressed in your skating. It will be . . . exquisite. Now skate, Jimmy Dean. Think on your wish."

The music begins as Peanut waves me out onto the ice. To the strain of U-2's "One" I begin my routine at center ice. By Svetlana, an aching, heaving melange of twisted body breakage and ruin. The small part of me deep down inside screams louder as I hasten into my routine. Crowds of emotionally moved Peanuts blink and weep peanut butter tears as I whir about the rink.

You were right, my Svetlana. My sweet Torvill. You foresaw the puzzle, the lady-or-the-tiger choice that I would be offered. Yet there is hope for the Pumpkin King's Sally in this living nightmare. I skate faster now, confidently easing deeper into my program as the thin ice of doubt thickens into resolution, the voice inside of me resonating downward from primal scream to a steady keening. For the choice has been determined. It remains only for the asking. I will have them rebuild you, my Svetlana. I will give you that ruby.

We will dance together among the stars.

Ritchie Feels All Right

"He'll give me a few minutes, then?"

Chandler sipped slowly from his Holiday Inn bar mai-tai, paused for some sort of imagined effect before barking in his annoying, seal-like laugh, then replied. "Oh, he'll give you a few, my friend, he will. Course, it wasn't easy convincing him, but I do have my ways. Old sod lad to old sod lad, y'know." Chandler winked and drained the last of his mai-tai, loudly smacked his lips and slapped his hands palm-down hard on the rickety lounge table that teetered between us. "You'll be famous, Roy, you will, after this interview."

I lightly sipped from my cup of Earl Grey tea and stared stone-faced at Chandler, speaking evenly. "There's potential interest in an anniversary article, for sure. Like I told you on the phone, Wenner's interested in a freelance piece for the Euro edition of *Rolling Stone*, but no one's bit on this side of the pond. Let's not forget, they never caught on big in the States."

I quietly placed my own hands palm-down on the table facing Chandler's, waited patiently for my emotional friend's reaction. He briefly stared at my fingers, then glancing up at my face broke into gales of maniacal seal laughter. Chandler suddenly stopped laughing and leaned forward, gazing intently into my eyes. I matched his stare.

"Look, Roy my boy, I know you too well. You were one of the few who followed the scene back then from Stateside, who really *tried* to get the British Invasion to stick amongst the U.S. Kids! You remember like I do that it was a complete mania at the time, both on the continent and the old sod! That feeling, that rush when it first took hold over there-it's worth at least a little peek back to all that for the Stateside crowd these days, innit?"

I shook my head slowly and seriously from side-to-side. "You're not listening, boy-o. I strictly cover the European scene for the Euro's entertainment. That's where the freelance money is. That's where the readership is. And, I'm afraid to say, that's where the heart of rock 'n roll resides, these days. Over there."

Chandler's face crimsoned with either rage or hurt or a mix of both, I wasn't really sure. Not for the first time, I wondered for a peek down the psychological well of my British expatriate friend, still so burning to somehow steer the music of his youth toward his adopted American masses. He stared down at his white-knuckled fists and seemed to work hard for a silent moment just to stay in control. Then with a world-weary sigh he reached down to the floor on his side of the table. His hands came up holding an old four track reel-to-reel tape recorder.

"Still restoring antiques, I gather."

Chandler winked and slightly smiled. "Mister Starkey suggested I lend you my latest restoration . . . a condition for the interview, actually. He likes my old recorders, lots of solid-state soul, you see. Bear with us on this one, you'll need it for your talk, tomorrow."

I shrugged compliance and reached for the recorder as Chandler stood to leave. "Be there at 10:15 a.m. Sharp. Mister Starkey has a work schedule to keep to. Oh, and one last thing, Roy."

"What's that?"

"He's a bit less formal, these days. You can call him Ritchie when you meet him. He actually prefers it to Mister Starkey or Richard."

"Then he's maybe feeling better about it all?"

Chandler snorted in disgust as he turned and walked away. "Yeah, right. A bloody lot better." He waved dismissively without looking back. Then I deliberately finished every last drop of my cold English tea.

At 10:05 a.m. I deposited my rented convertible in the Betty Ford Clinic parking lot. The Clinic receptionist advised me that Ritchie most likely just finished group and would be found in his usual break spot. I followed yellow signs and arrows through the complex and into the small clinic cafeteria. Ritchie idly looked up from his newspaper as I walked over to his quiet corner. He looked very relaxed and tan in well-worn cowboy boots, jeans and a loose maroon shirt, half-expired cigarette and styrofoam cup of tea in-hand. My heart caught in my throat as I saw in his middle-aged face the boy remembered from my own boyhood 35 years ago. He smiled with the same wide-eyed, kind expression from youth.

"You must be Chandler's friend Roy, now," he said softly, gesturing for me to pull up a cafeteria chair. "Help yourself to the tea canister and a cup."

I was somewhat taken aback by Ritchie's voice, the tone being the same as it was, with the accent pressed down thin by the weight of the years in America. He seemed to sense my reaction and lightly chuckled, took a long drag on his cigarette and smiled, politely waiting.

"I appreciate the time you've agreed to take as well as the opportunity to talk to you, Ritchie."

"I hope you're not too nervous, then," he replied.

I did relax a bit, buoyed by the familiar old voice. Even with the lessened accent, that old English way he always had of drawing-out pronunciation of a word like nervous. Ne-e-er-vous.

"Just a bit. After all, it is your first interview in 35 years."

Ritchie's expression shifted from happy-go-lucky to a suddenly wary look. "And a brief one at that," he said. "I don't know what Chandler told you, but two ground rules. I have another group to lead before the hour so that's it, time-wise. Also, you can record, but use the machine that Chandler lent you." He relaxed back into the old Ritchie as I nodded agreement, chuckled anew as I bent to connect thick plug to wall socket. "If the old machine was good enough for our media back then, it should be good enough for you, now."

"Which leads to my first question, Ritchie. After all the years of seclusion and lying low, why now?"

Ritchie dragged on the cigarette, exhaled a fine stream thoughtfully before slowly speaking. "I wouldn't call it seclusion now, would I? After all, I've been counseling stars and celebrities here at the Clinic for over eight years, now. At times it can be a regular media circus around here."

"True," I replied. "But you're not the center of the circus, here. In fact, you've been so low-key, you're not even a sideshow to the American media. So again, why here and now?"

Ritchie reached between us and picked up the tea canister, refilled his cup and poured a fresh one for me.

"That's a good point, then," he said after a sip. "First off, there's no way you can write a thorough article on the era without in some quiet manner at least brushing up against us. I read your short column in *Spin* a few year's back, '96 was it? I liked the way you alluded a bit of influence to us, at least." He took a longer pull at his tea. "And then of course, there's the timing of your article. Chandler's told me a lot about you. Personally, that is. Interesting time to write about the old days, innit? Given publication will be the anniversary month of the event, and all."

The Event.

It sat like a stark package on the table between us, waiting to be unwrapped by aging hands. I wrapped my own hands around my styrofoam cup in search of some form of fleeting warmth and solace.

"Look, Roy, I know from Chandler how much it all meant to you, then. And I don't have much time before break's over. So how about if you just sit and listen like an old fan, one of our few American ones, apparently, while I recount a bit my view of it all leading to the event. Then you can do what you want with it. Or not. All right?"

I nodded.

"Gear, then," said Ritchie, lighting a fresh cigarette.

"We were riding high in late '63, Fall it was. I'd been with the lads for a little over a year, since Pete left, and the mania for us was at full throttle on the continent and home in England. That's when two new ideas popped up. First, an executive at United Artists came up with the movie concept. No rock group had ever made a truly successful transition from the concert stage to the sound stage. We trusted Brian's advice and he trusted his instincts. And his instincts said to go for it.

"The idea would be to do a musical, with eight or nine new songs written by John and Paul just for the picture. We wanted to show a typical day in our lives, with the goal of escaping from the mania of our own success. We wanted to break through the mania, emphasize in different movie sequences our individual personalities, have our fans truly see us as people. John as the sarcastic, quick-witted leader. Paul as the cute, clever peacemaker. George with his wry, shy humor. And me, I suppose. Always in the back, always separate, but all the girl's favorite.

"We really warmed to the idea, what with Brian committing Richard Lester to direct. He did *The Goon Show* on British telly at the time, Peter Sellars old show, and we felt he'd be perfect for our style of comedy, the touch of surrealistic humor we wanted to bring to the film. The plan was to begin shooting in Twickenham Studios over the winter of '64 and we were all gear for it. Then Brian and John get it in their fool heads for us to postpone it for an American tour, of all things.

"I remember Paul expressing our mutual uncertainty to John and Brian. Epstein hadn't been able to show us any proof that our form of music was very popular over here, what with your Vice-President McCarthy's attitude toward 'imports' so generally pervasive, even among the kids. 'Think about it,' John crowed. 'We'll be the second British invasion of the States!' 'Second British Dunkirk's more like it,' I remember Paul shooting back. 'What with their un-American or non-American or bloody whatever attitude over there, I not only think they'll hate us but I won't feel safe over there!' We argued through the night and of course, John being John, he converted Paul just enough to get him to turn the other cheek, with George and I reluctantly riding Paul's coattails.

"We landed in New York in February and you know the rest. Nixon just couldn't control his Vice-President's oratorical venom toward us during the week before we arrived. After the anti-British riot at the airport, we were definitely throwing-in the towel, heading back to friendlier climes. Brian had a late afternoon press conference scheduled at the hotel to announce cancellation of our appearance on The Ed Sullivan Show. We were all looking forward to John telling McCarthy at the press conference to bugger off. It was just pure bad karma when that bloody bastard shot John in the lobby on the way to the conference."

"Thank God it was just a flesh wound," I interjected.

Ritchie shrugged. "Who knows, maybe a kinder fate would've let it all end quickly and cleanly right then."

"You can't honestly mean that."

Ritchie shook his head. "Now you see, my friend, that's where you've got it all wrong. The John that we all knew and loved did expire that day. The weeks leading from our return home from New York to the event proved otherwise. Let me ask you something. You've seen the footage, have you? Chandler said you did. He showed you the reels one evening just after the two of you left the service."

"I did," I replied, feeling as if I'd been caught with something I'd shoplifted.

"It's o.k.," said Ritchie. "Tell me, whatever just pops into your head right now, what did you think of them? What was your immediate reaction?"

The answer came easily enough. "I had the feeling that you were all having fun. There was such a wonderful sense of spontaneity to the scenes."

Ritchie smiled sadly. "That was the general idea of the thing. We even had this gear movie title. Sometimes when we were up recording all night we'd all be dragging the next day and I'd say to John, 'boy, that was a hard day's night.' John loved the expression, insisted that we were going to call the completed film 'A Hard Day's Night.' We all loved it, it fit the hoped for mood perfectly."

I once again found myself sipping cold English tea. "Only once again fate randomly intervened."

"Randomly, my ass," said Ritchie firmly.

"What exactly do you mean," I asked carefully.

"Let me ask you another question," Ritchie replied. "Again, regarding the movie scenes. Think what I told you, and then think what you saw. Now what's missing from those scenes?"

I thought for a moment and then it came to me. "It was supposed to be a musical. I know it's unedited footage and all, but there aren't any musical scenes. The event must have happened before you could film them."

"Correction, my friend. The event occurred *because* we couldn't film them."

"I don't understand."

"It's very simple. Like I said earlier, the idea was for John and Paul to cobble together eight or nine new songs for the film and an accompanying soundtrack record. Only that gunshot back in Manhattan took out more than just some superficial arm flesh. It took out John's creative heart."

Ritchie angrily stabbed a cigarette out on the table and tossed the butt into his cup. "No matter how tough and smart-assed he seemed on the surface, underneath John was the most sensitive of the lads, the most idealistic. Paul saw that in him and that's why they wrote so well together. Regardless of his press conference intentions, John loved America, he wanted our music to reach the people and change the bitter feelings that prevailed in those days among Americans toward the rest of the world. The movie and the music wouldn't be political, but would teach people, particularly Americans, how to react to an ossified country around them, to treat each other better and consequently the world.

"The music died that day in New York. John was more emotionally shattered when we got home than outsiders realized. And the film shooting schedule was so tight, only seven weeks, really. And there was none of it left inside John. No drive, no creative anger, no quick sarcasm. Just a big, bleeding, jilting ache. That the world could come to this. He knew it and we knew it. And Paul couldn't carry it alone, never mind poor quiet George.

"And then John made the event."

I stared dumb-founded at Ritchie, barely able to breathe.

"Come now, lad," he said softly. "You didn't think I invited you here to reminisce after 35 years about a random accident, did you?"

My reporter's instinct couldn't rise, held down by my feelings as a loving fan. So Ritchie just sighed and continued.

"Like all films, this one's scenes are shot out of the planned final sequence. So we're about halfway through and we're scheduled to shoot the final scripted scene. We're supposed to run from our successful concert out into a nearby field and into a big old early sixties helicopter transport, which takes off dropping leaflets of us. The end.

"Now things were as bloody low as they could get before this scene. And still absolutely no music. No new songs. A complete, dreary drag. The day before we had shot that happy-go-lucky scene of us running around like puppies in a field and John hadn't even shown up.

"But John suddenly shows up for the helicopter scene. Brian's ecstatic, raving how he seems like the old John, at last. But I can see something's forced, something's eerie in'em. And I can also see it in Paul and George. And I'm definitely sensing that the lads are leaving me out on something. I'd gotten that feeling before, you know. Mind you, they'd been together a long time before I came along.

"So we do the helicopter scene. We rush in, the door closes. We go up and the leaflets fall. And that's a take.

"Only John doesn't let it go. He tells us and Lester that he wants one more take, a prank shot for an outtake party. I'm feeling funny about it but he gets all heated, says he just wants a funny favor. 'Don't you worry,' he said to me, 'I'll push Paul out first, he's the prettiest.' So I go along with the lad."

Ritchie paused a moment and leaned back. "You've seen the reel. Tell me what you saw."

I swallowed. "Paul and George hop into the helicopter. You're about to climb in when John trips you to the ground from behind. John bends over you, then stands and jumps over you. He turns and salutes the camera. As you start to get to your feet, he hops in and slams the door shut. You fall out of camera range as the coptor climbs. The camera follows the coptor as it goes high.

Much higher than in the earlier take. Then slowly spins. Then falls. Then explodes."

"I'll always wonder how he caused it. But I'll never wonder why."

"You have no proof," I croaked.

"Like I said, my lads were eerie that day. I believe it was agreement I was sensin', although I'm sure that John was the leader. I was the only one who could ever play it all for laughs, who could see the light at the end of the tunnel. Beyond the mania. Beyond the American hurt and the songwriting dysfunction. But it was too much for them. And like I said, they'd been together for a long time. A lifetime, really. So John made his own tunnel for my lads, with a special light at the end of it."

We sat in silence for awhile in the now empty cafeteria. The wall clock hands slowly neared toward Ritchie's next group. I reached beyond my teacup and snapped the old recorder off.

"You can't expect me to write this."

"Of course I do," Ritchie said. "But that's not why you're here."

Ritchie went on in answer to my uncomprehending look. "I've two British gifts for you. But first, one final film question. When John bent over me the moment after he tripped me, what do you think he said?"

"The thought hadn't really occurred. With his back to the camera, one can't tell if he said anything at all. It looked like he was just quickly checking on you."

"Oh, he said something, all right." Ritchie reached under his abandoned newspaper and slid out to me a large manila envelope. "He was bloody quick about it. He said 'I left you a last bit of us back at the hotel.' Then he hopped onboard. I found this under my pillow. Later."

I opened the envelope and slid-out an old four-track tape box. Inside of it was an old four-track reel tape with a folded note. I unfolded the note and read:

R.-

> I had one last banger in me, most likely the title song. But getting it out burnt me to ash. A real hard day's night, this one. But you'll raise it someday, like a phoenix from these wet ashes. When the time is right. You'll know when.
>
> Love,
>
> -J.

I looked up through my tears at a confident Ritchie. "A real banger, it is. He must've done it that day when the rest of us were prancin' like fools in that field.

"The time is right, Roy. The old attitudes have faded cold. It'll have it's effect, today, in America. I know it will. Give it to the right people. They'll listen and they'll know what to do with it."

Ritchie looked toward the wall clock as I quickly wiped my eyes, then we both stood as he gathered his newspaper together.

"You said you had something else for me."

Ritchie laughed. "Yeah, right." He picked up the tea canister and poured the last of the steaming tea into a fresh cup, then handed it to me. "Chandler was right about your cold tea habit. Such penance! Here's a hot one for the road. And a bit of Liverpool advice. Don't drink it cold. Only revenge should be taken cold. And there's no real satisfaction innit, is there? We're all beyond that, now. I learned that here, first as a guest and then as a staffer."

I smiled and took a sip as we reached the corridor. Ritchie halted. "One last thing."

"Anything."

"You're the reporter, and I asked all the questions. So just for old time's sake, if you've one quick question I've got a moment for it."

It crawled out onto my tongue, from where I don't know. "Like they used to ask you in the old days. Do you have anything you'd like to say to your fans?"

He smiled sweetly and innocently, the old Liverpool lad momentarily rejuvenated. "Listen to the tape, Roy. Then tell them

Ritchie Starkey . . . tell them Ringo feels all right . . . you know, I feel all right."

Then he turned and walked off down the corridor to go help others.